Sweeter Than Sin

Dangerous Liaisons — Book 2

BESTSELLING AUTHOR

ANDREA PICKENS

OLIVERHEBERBOOKS

CHAPTER 1

Fire. Smoke. The lush scent of sweetness licking up from the flames.

"Breathe deeply, Rafael." The contessa held him close to the swirling steam. "Drink in its essence." She sprinkled a grating of cinnamon, a pinch of anchiote over the roasting nibs. "Watch carefully, *querida*. Like life itself, the cacao is even better with a bit of spice, but the mix must be just right. Let me show you."

Her hands fluttered over the copper cauldron, still quick and graceful despite the gnarled knuckles and fragile wrists. "*Theobroma cacao*—food of the gods," she said. "Now we must wait for just the right moment to douse the flames. Remember, its magic cannot be rushed, Rafael."

From a smaller pot, the contessa poured a measure of hot milk into a silver cup. Adding a spoonful of ground beans, thickened with sugar, she whipped the concoction to a foaming froth with her *molinillo*. "But patience will be rewarded. Drink this."

Throat parched, Rafael de Villefranca Greeley managed only a hoarse croak as he grabbed at thin air.

"Drink this, sir." The sergeant dodged a fist and held the glass to the major's lips. "The doctor says it will help ease the pain."

Now fully awake, Rafael fell back against the rumpled pillow. The laudanum was bitter as bile on his tongue. Not at all like the taste of his grandmother's chocolate. He closed his eyes, savoring for an instant the spicy warmth of her laughter, the touch of her sugar-dusted fingers upon his cheek.

Sweet memories.

But now there was only opium, and a darkness blacker than hell.

He gulped down a swallow and waited for the drug to dull his senses. Shadows flickered in the guttering candlelight of the field hospital, ghostly patterns on the bloodstained canvas. From nearby, a man moaned, his agony echoing down the row of straw pallets.

"You are lucky to be alive, sir," said the sergeant. "An English officer pulled you from beneath your dying horse before the French could muster a counterattack."

Am I?

The shapes blurred, and the frail fingers of the elderly countess curved into sabers. Slashing steel, filling the air with the stench of death. A splash of crimson as his cousin spurred forward to block the blow meant for his own head. Pressing his palms to his brow, Rafael bit back a groan. His skin was sheened in sweat and yet he was chilled to the bone.

Jack was dead and he was alive. That was no blessing but a curse. How was he ever to face his uncle with the news?

Shivering, Rafael surrendered to oblivion, knowing it was a coward's way out of the battle. But even as he sunk into a fitful sleep, he knew the war was far from over.

"WHY MUST you always be so cautious?"

"Because one of us must try to temper wild spirits with common sense."

Kyra Sterling colored, uncomfortably aware that her sister's words held more than a grain of truth. At the moment, however, the warning rubbed raw. She ducked to tighten the saddle girth. "You needn't come along, Lexy. I'm more than willing to bear the brunt of any trouble that comes from this." The big stallion whinnied as she worked the bit between his teeth. "Not that there is much chance of that. Aunt Adelaide is dozing in a corner of the card room—"

"You ought not to have slipped brandy into her punch," chided Alexandra.

"It's a harmless prank." Kyra's laugh, slightly slurred by several glasses of champagne, gave way to a defiant little tilt of her chin. "Chas bet Harry that I could not ride Pemberton's bay to the abbey ruins and back in under a quarter of an hour. What fun I shall have in making him eat his words."

"But the way leads close by the river. Mr. Talley says the recent rains have made the banks treacherously unstable."

"Lud, don't be such a stick in the mud," she muttered under her breath.

Alexandra's expression turned even grimmer on seeing Kyra lift her skirts. "Oh, surely you can't mean to ride *astride*!

"And why not?" Lord Matherton waggled a brow as he looked into the stall. In the flickering lantern light, his hair gleamed gold though his face was wreathed in shadow. "Your sister shows an exceedingly lovely ankle."

"Which a gentleman ought not to encourage her to expose," replied Alexandra sharply.

"Oh, come now." Matherton flicked a bit of straw from his coat. The navy superfine clung to his shoulders, accentuating the slope of muscle and breadth of his chest. "As an engaged couple, we are allowed to bend the rules just a touch, don't you think?"

Kyra felt a lick of heat as his gaze ran up the length of her legs.

Alexandra's lips thinned.

Ignoring the silent reproach, she slid the flounced silk a bit higher. "Have you come to wish me luck, Chas?"

He caught her up in his arms and kissed her full on the mouth. "I know how well you ride a stallion, m'dear." A wicked gleam lit his eye. "But be warned. I shall claim a forfeit if you lose."

"And what is that?" she teased.

Matherton nipped at the lobe of her ear. His breath was hot, the spice of her father's aged brandy still lush on his lips. "Oh, I think you can guess."

Her face began to burn. Thank God her sister could not see her flaming cheeks or the press of the viscount's thighs against hers.

"You like playing with fire, don't you, sweeting?

"Oh, yes," she whispered, fisting at the fastenings of his shirt. His jaw was smooth as marble. Like a Greek God. A paragon of sculpted perfection. And in another two months, he would be her husband. Surely, it was not so very wanton to take pleasure in the passion that sizzled between them.

Forbidden pleasures. There were rules, of course, about passion. But rules were meant to be broken.

"So do I, Kyra." Her fiancé's eyes were heavy-lidded with desire. "So do I." Hands hard on her waist, he swung her up to the saddle. The stallion shied at the flapping fabric, but Matherton gripped the bridle.

"Harry has already saddled our mounts."

He was no longer whispering but his voice still held an intimate note. "I trust you don't mind if we come along for the ride?"

Kyra set her slippers in the stirrups. Her thigh, bare but for stockings, gripped the cool leather. It was shockingly sensual, like Matherton's grin.

"Are you up to the challenge?" he continued. "I dare—"

"I'm coming, too." Alexandra turned abruptly and pulled down a sidesaddle from the stable racks.

"Lexy, I don't need a . . ." Kyra hesitated, unsure of what she meant to say. *A guardian? A conscience?*

"The more, the merrier," drawled Matherton. His hand touched lightly to the curve of her knee. "But let us hurry before one of your father's grooms raises a hue and cry."

"They are well used to me rebelling against my father's rules." Kyra laughed. She was no longer a child but a woman on the verge of marriage. One last kicking up of her heels could do no harm. "And seeing as he won't return from Town until tomorrow evening, no one will grass on us."

Out in the stable yard, a pale sliver of moon afforded little light. Kyra gathered her reins, giving thanks that she knew the way by heart.

"On the count of three!" called Harry, snapping his pocket watch shut.

A slap of her crop sent the big bay thundering past the paddocks. Leaning low, Kyra cut across the open field and headed for the cart path. Neck and neck with Matherton's mount, she angled for the opening in the copse of trees. Branches whipped at her face and legs. Above the pounding hooves, she thought she heard her gown rip.

She laughed, giddy with the thrill of throwing all restraint to the wind. Her heart was racing, echoing the wild delight pulsing through her veins.

The world seemed to stretch out before her. She felt so utterly, gloriously alive.

Out of the corner of her eye, she caught a glimpse of Matherton grinning like the very devil. Lud, his looks still took her breath away. She knew she was the envy of every young lady in Town. His polished charm and angelic looks more than made up for a modest fortune and title. After all, her family's prestige would open any doors, and her dowry was enough to keep them living in splendor for half a dozen lifetimes.

As for his skills at lovemaking . . .

Her hands tightened on the reins. She had heard rumors of his rakish exploits, but all young gentlemen were wont to be wild. He had promised her that he was reformed.

"Slow down, Kyra!" Alexandra's cry was nearly drowned by the rush of water.

But she was not about to heed the appeal. Matherton was already a length ahead of her and gaining ground.

The path dipped sharply, threading through gorse and heather before taking one last turn at the river's edge. She peered ahead. A narrow straightaway, then a short climb to the crest of the hill.

A flick of her crop urged the lathered stallion to greater speed. She could pick up a precious second or two—

"Kyra!"

Suddenly, the earth began to crumble beneath the flying hooves. Panicking, the big bay tried to rear, only to have its back legs buckle in the slippery mud.

A scream—not her own.

Kyra tried to kick free of the stirrups, but her skirts had become too tangled in the tack.

A searing pain.

And then everything went black.

CHAPTER 2

Rafael spun the *molinillo* between his palms. The wooden whisk, darkened to a rich patina by melted chocolate, seemed so much smaller than he remembered.

He set it aside and picked up the small ivory miniature of his grandmother. *Ah, but Dona Maria would always seem larger than life.* A ghost of a smile played on his lips. Earthy yet otherworldly. Imperious, yet impish. Her penchant for black only added to her aura of mystery—midnight silks and lace mantillas, ebony hair combs and jet jewelry. He suspected she relished her reputation among the local peasants as a sorceress with healing powers.

"Chocolate," she replied, when he had once asked her the source of her magic. "Indeed, *querida*, Aztec legend has it that the god Quetzalcoatl descended from heaven on a beam of the morning star, carrying a cacao tree stolen from Paradise."

Rafael stared out the window. When he had repeated the tale to his father, John Richard Greeley had sighed and warned him that he must take the dowager contessa's stories with a grain of salt. Greeley was English, of course, his cool reason and fair good looks a marked contrast to Dona Maria's Spanish fire and smoky beauty. The two were warm friends, yet elementally different. *Sugar and spice.* Even as a child he had sensed it.

He caught his own reflection in the mullioned glass. His raven locks and olive complexion had come from his Spanish mother, while his ice-blue eyes and square jaw bespoke his Anglo Saxon heritage.

Two opposing natures? He made a wry face. Was it any wonder that he felt conflicted about a great many things these days?

Paper crackled as Rafael took a bulging portfolio from his grandmother's trunk and untied the ribbons. Skimming the top page, he smiled again.

Combine two measures of sun-dried criolla beans with a handful of trinitaros. Grind to a fine paste on a heated (very important) metate, adding sugar from Barbados, nutmeg from Martinique and the dried seeds of one vanilla bean. (Use only those from Madagascar! They are far more flavorful than the Mexican variety . . .

Recipes. A peek inside several of the other matching cases showed copious notes on the cacao plant. Dona Maria had devoted much of her life to collecting information about her beloved beans. Lore, legend, historical fact—each new tidbit was meticulously transcribed in her spidery script.

Chocolate was her passion, and she had always intended to write a book on the subject. As Rafael read over her instructions for making a breakfast beverage, he couldn't help thinking, *Lud, what a volume that would have been.*

But war had ripped through Spain, tearing such dreams asunder. Her powers, however magical, could not halt the advance of the French army. Nor could they keep the mountain cart path from crumbling under the wheels of the family carriage as it sought to pass over the Pyrenees. He pressed the paper to his cheek, breathing in the faint traces of her perfume. She had perished in the crash, leaving him with naught but bittersweet memories.

Smoothing at the scrap of paper, Rafael was unashamed of the tears clinging to his lashes. English gentlemen were forbidden to cry, he knew. It was considered unmanly to express emotion. *A stiff upper lip.* His grandmother had clucked in disapproval at the English notion of *sang froid*, saying it was harmful to feelings bottled up inside. He had been twelve years old when his parents had succumbed to an epidemic of influenza. Dona Maria had held him in her arms that night, saying it was only natural to give voice to his sorrow and fears. Come morning, the two of them had shared a soothing cup of her special chocolate.

She had taught him much about life.

After a moment, Rafael put the portfolios back in the trunk and carefully refastened the silver clasps. The past was the past. However grim the future appeared, he must not look back.

The present was difficult enough to face. His gaze strayed to the smaller wooden box. Duty demanded that he deliver his cousin Jack's personal effects to his uncle in Kent, along with a first-hand account of the young man's heroism. Like himself, the elderly earl was now the sole survivor of his immediate family. And though the two of them had met only occasionally, Rafael felt compelled to offer more than an impersonal letter.

His leg nearly buckled as he rose. The saber cut had healed, but there were still shards of shrapnel embedded in his flesh. However, physical discomfort was the least of his concerns. The pain of the coming journey was going to pierce far deeper into flesh and blood.

Sighing, he marked an *X* on the lid of Jack's trunk. The carters would soon arrive to take his luggage to the ship. His grandmother's papers would be left behind in a warehouse, along with other items rescued from the family hacienda. He was leaving on the evening tide. Maybe one day . . .

As he turned away, the chalk slipped from his fingers. It bounced off the silver hinge of Dona Maria's trunk, spun in a slow circle through the air and fell back against the ebony wood, somehow inscribing identical intersecting lines across its surface.

Rafael swore and leaned down to erase them. But at the last instant, something held him back.

On second thought, given his unsteady gait, he was likely to be cooped up for much of the sea voyage in his cabin. Reading through the notes certainly would help pass the hours. She had accumulated a wealth of arcane knowledge, like the fact that ancient Aztec warriors drank chocolate in order to fortify their stamina during battle.

Strength from chocolate? A fanciful notion.

But then, his grandmother had a fanciful imagination. Her presence, if only in pen and ink, would be a soothing balm for his aching spirit.

"SURELY THERE IS something you can do!" The duke's appeal was perilously close to a shout.

"You are understandably upset, Your Grace," said his companion.

The duke's scowl deepened, but he looked more harried than angry.

Poor Papa. Kyra slipped a step closer to the half open door. No wonder he appeared on the brink of despair. She had been a sore trial to him ever since she was in leading strings. Little arms and legs tugging, tumbling in every direction. Tying things in a terrible tangle. Even back then, she had chafed at any restraint on her actions.

She had always thought of herself as high-spirited rather than willful. Bold rather than reckless. It was only now that she understood the dangers of self-deception.

"I've consulted every blasted specialist on Harley Street," continued the duke. "They are all charlatans! I might just as well have spent my blunt on the traveling quacks who peddle elixirs from their pushcarts." He drew in a harsh breath. "But you,

Professor McTavish, your credentials are above reproach. The University of St. Andrews is known for its excellence in medicine."

The Scottish doctor clasped his hands behind his back. "You are wasting your guineas on me as well, Your Grace, if you expect me to work a miracle cure."

Kyra liked McTavish even more for his blunt honesty. Of all the medical men who had poked and prodded at her body, he was the only one who seemed to understand where the real injuries lay.

"But—" began Pierpont.

"Her leg is healing quite nicely. The truth is, other than the broken bone, there is nothing really wrong with your daughter."

Her father's eyes widened in disbelief. "The devil there isn't. She won't eat! She barely speaks!"

Kyra bit at her lip.

"As I said, there is nothing physically wrong with your daughter. As for her state of mind . . ."

The color leached from the duke's face. He whispered an oath. "You think the fall has damaged her wits?"

"No, not at all. The symptoms you describe are not uncommon in this situation. Indeed, they are especially apt to occur in young ladies." McTavish stroked his chin. "You say that Lady Kyra's sister was killed in the same riding accident that resulted in her own injuries?"

"Yes."

"Likely she blames herself for the mishap."

"My nephew, who played a regrettable role in the dare, did say that Alexandra tried to warn Kyra of the danger," replied her father.

"Ah." Removing his spectacles, the doctor pinched the bridge of his nose.

Kyra did not wait to hear anything more. Stepping back from her hiding place, she limped the length of the corridor and quietly closed the door of her workroom. Solitude was her only solace these days.

The duke, however, stood still as stone, anxiously waiting for the doctor to go on. Coals crackled in the hearth. A log snapped. From its perch on the mantel, an ormolu clock chimed the hour. As the last ring died away, he slapped a palm to the polished marble.

"Well? What do you prescribe?"

"Patience. Understanding."

Skepticism arched Pierpont's brow. "You are suggesting that platitudes can cure what ails her?"

The doctor smiled. "Sometimes love is the best medicine of all."

~

"RAFAEL." The wrinkled hands were warm, welcoming as they framed his face. Lips, dry as parchment, kissed his cheeks. "Welcome, welcome. Your mother always insisted that I greet you in the Spanish way. But it has been a long time—I trust I am not making a hash of it."

"Not at all, Uncle Aubrey. You make me feel very much at home."

"Hendrie Hall is your home now, Rafael. For as long as you like."

"Thank you, sir." He followed the earl into the entrance hall, his steps slow and deliberate to hide the stiffness of his leg.

"I am delighted you accepted my invitation." Hendrie looked back, a sad smile on his face. "I hope you will not find yourself growing too bored. We have none of the glitter or the gaiety of Town entertainments here in the country. And the only company I can offer you is that of two spoiled hounds and a rather dull old man."

And ghosts. Rafael stared up at the two portraits hanging above the side table. He had never met his English grandparents, but he saw much of his father in the late earl and countess. The curve of the lips, the shape of a chin, that angle of a brow, and yet, no artist, however skilled, could capture the sound of laughter, the wink of an eye.

No wonder his uncle looked so pale and drawn. Living with only paint and canvas for company was no substitute for flesh and blood family. Despite his own pain, he was glad he had come.

"Peace and quiet is just what I desire, sir. The moors and meadows of Hendrie Hall offer ample opportunity to partake of the fresh air and exercise prescribed by the doctors. And I recall that you have a splendid library."

"Ah, yes, that is right. You are a scholar as well as a soldier." The earl drew in a long breath. "Jack did not care much for books. I am so pleased that the Hendrie collection will afford some measure of enjoyment to a member of the family."

"I look forward to spending many hours exploring its treasures."

"It gives me some measure of solace to know that it will go to you, who appreciates it." The earl's expression brightened. "First, I ought to reacquaint you with the labyrinth layout of the manor. I have put you in the rooms overlooking the Orangerie." As the footmen passed by with the luggage from the traveling coach, his smile stretched a touch wider. "I recognize that distinctive design of scrolled silver and polished ebony. Dona Maria was a remarkable lady. No one could match her sense of style."

"Or flair for the fantastical," said Rafael dryly. "At times it drove Father to distraction."

"A unique character, to be sure," chuckled Hendrie. "You must remind me to tell you of the time she insisted on cooking a Christmas dinner here at the Hall, a feast that included goose sauced with all manner of exotic ingredients—including chocolate."

"Her famous Mexican mole," Rafael said.

"Whatever its name, it caused the French cook to quit in a huff. No great loss, I must add, as we were all growing tired of overcooked roast beef." His uncle watched the last wink of silver disappear around a bend in the stairway. "If Dona Maria had been English, she would have been called an Original."

"In any language, she was always described as a lady of bold imagination."

"I am glad to see you have some tangible reminder of her to carry with you."

"Her papers survived," explained Rafael. "It may be only a fanciful notion, but I have been thinking about editing her research and recipes on chocolate into a book."

"What a splendid idea!" exclaimed his uncle. "There are a number of volumes on botany in the library that may prove useful, as well as some histories on the early explorations of the New World." Warming to the subject, he added, "And Lord Silliman, head of the Royal Botanical Society, is an old friend. I am sure he could offer excellent advice on a publisher."

"I have only begun to sort through her notes, but the possibilities seem intriguing."

"Indeed, indeed. Is there anything else you might need for the project?"

Rafael thought for a moment. "Perhaps a place outdoors where I might sit for several hours when the weather is favorable. I have spent too much time confined in places where the sun could not shine and . . ." He let his voice trail off.

"I know just the spot." Like a breeze rustling through autumn leaves, Hendrie's reply had a faint crackle to it.

Rafael worried that perhaps he had stirred up painful memories, but the earl went on with unmistakable enthusiasm.

"There is a folly by the lake, a rather overwrought interpretation of Greek architecture, but its marble roof and fluted columns afford excellent protection from the elements. When he was a child, Jack used it as a boathouse for his pond yachts, and there are still several comfortable benches and a large stone slab at one end of the terrace that serves as a table."

"It sounds ideal."

"The views out over the moors are lovely, especially at sunset. And if you wish to walk, you will find a number of trails through the surrounding forests and fields. Other than the occasional hare or hawk, you are not likely to encounter any intrusion on your solitude."

"That suits me just fine, sir. I assure you, I am not looking for amusements." As for a more meaningful search? Rafael was not even sure he could put into words what he was after.

His uncle seemed to sense his hesitation and did not press for further explanation. "Come then, let me see you settled in your quarters. I shall show you through the rest of the Hall before supper. Afterward, we may take our brandy in the library where I can explain the quirks of how the collection is cataloged. The third earl was a noted eccentric."

"I am used to eccentrics in the family."

They shared a quick smile before the earl turned and started up the stairs under the watchful gaze of a gallery of illustrious ancestors.

Old and young.

How quickly time marched by, thought Rafael as he followed his uncle. A lifetime passing in the blink of an eye. For an instant, he envied the paintings. Pigment and canvas felt no grief, no heartache, no regrets. But then he looked away, reminding himself that neither had they ever experienced Dona Maria's laughter, or the sublime sweetness of her chocolate at midnight.

Steadying his steps on the sweeping banister, he passed by a youthful Jack perched on a pony and hurried through the paneled portals that led to the family wing of the manor house.

~

ADDING a drop of ochre to the pool of alizarin crimson, Kyra dipped her brush in the swirl of pigment and drew in a shadow. Another stroke deepened the petal's hue, and another sketched in a line of shading beneath a furled bud.

Satisfied, she leaned back from her easel and set about mixing a range of reds—from a pale peach to a deep flame. The freshly picked rose was lush with nuanced color and velvety textures. She would have to work quickly before the bloom faded.

"It's lovely."

Kyra turned slowly.

Her father stood in the doorway, looking awkward, unsure.

The duke in doubt? If only she might keep all the pain to herself.

He peered at the watercolor then cleared his throat. "Grimsell says your work is good enough to hang in the Royal Botanical Society's annual exhibit."

She rinsed her brush and carefully twisted the sable hairs to a fine point. "He is being kind, but I don't think I am anywhere near ready for such a step."

"No need to rush your fences." He paled as the riding term slipped from his lips. "What I meant was ..."

"I know what you meant, Papa. It's just that, I have no desire to be a part of Society."

"But you will," he whispered. "In due time."

Kyra did not answer right away. Her maid, ever loyal, had taken it upon herself to eavesdrop on Lord Matherton's recent visit to the duke's study. Oh, how quickly her fiancé's façade of sculpted perfection had shown its flaws.

Apparently a lengthy postponement of the nuptials, not to speak of a limping bride, did not quite suit the viscount's plans. He had cried off from the engagement. And to cover his own ungentlemanly behavior—Society was very strict on rules governing a man's going back on his word—he had excused himself by mentioning rumors concerning her virtue. He had been clever in manipulating the facts, the incidents, with witnesses to corroborate them, had just enough truth in them to stand up to scrutiny, and they pointed to the harsh reality that she was indeed a broken vessel.

So, her reputation, like the rest of her life, lay in ruins, while Matherton, who was equally guilty, had escaped with a nary a scratch.

Love. To think she had ever believed in its magic.

"I fear not, Papa. I know Lord Matherton has broken off our engagement. Just as I know of the whispers that are swirling through Town."

His jaw tightened. "I'll have his guts for garters."

"But they have a grain of truth to them, Father." Kyra forced herself to meet his eyes. "Yet another burden you must bear on my account."

The duke sat heavily upon the edge of her worktable.

"I was a fool," she whispered. "Too vain and too selfish to see aught but my own desires. I am so very sorry for everything."

"Who?" rasped the duke.

Kyra gave a small shake of her head. "It is not important. The real fault is mine. If only . . ."

If only. She could fill of ream of foolscap with a litany of regrets.

"Mistakes can be forgiven, Kyra."

"Not when it comes to a lady's honor." Her hand closed around the stem of the rose, the thorns pricking deep into her flesh. "I have sown the seeds of my own disgrace by earning a reputation for wildness. People are more than willing to think the worst."

"True friends will stand by you." The duke reached out and gently uncurled her fingers from the flower. He held her for a moment and then brushed a caress to her cheek. His callused palm was surprisingly warm.

"I am not sure I deserve their loyalty. Or yours."

"Nonsense," he said gruffly. "You will see that Dr. McTavish is right—time heals all."

It would take a far more potent balm than time to heal her wounds, but she did not have the heart to say so aloud.

Brushing a few of the fallen petals from his breeches, the duke stood and gave a wry smile. "I am afraid I have destroyed the subject of your study."

"No matter. I shall fetch a fresh rose and a blank sheet of paper and start over." Would that it was so easy to correct life's mishaps.

Kyra waited until her father's steps faded away before allowing a stifled sob. Tears pearled on her lashes. "I wish I had died instead of Lexy," she whispered. "Everyone would be happier for it."

CHAPTER 3

"*Deciduo.*" Gazing up at the skies, Rafael added an oath in Spanish. "*Diablo*! What is the English word—dessi . . . dessa . . . desser . . ?" he demanded of the hawk circling overhead.

The bird's effortless flight seemed a mocking reflection of his struggles with language. With a lazy flap of its wings, it soared higher, then disappeared in the mist of the distant moors.

On the morrow, he must remember to bring a dictionary. As well as another notebook and extra pencils. Glancing at the unruly piles of paper spread over the stone slab, he heaved a sigh. The task was proving even more daunting than he had first imagined. Though his English was excellent, his knowledge of botany was only rudimentary, so he was having a devil of a time translating Dona Maria's notes on the different varieties of her beloved beans.

"*Cacao theobroma, Theobroma sterculiaceae.*" he muttered, looking down at the note in his lap. "What do you call such bloody trees?"

"Deciduous." The reply seemed to come out of nowhere.

His head jerked up. "What?"

Straight ahead, the marble columns stood silent. Rafael looked to the lake and saw only a ripple of wind stirring the placid waters. *Ghosts.* In both word and pictures, he was surrounded by vivid reminders of the past. Was it any wonder that his imagination was playing tricks on him? Chiding himself for such flights of fancy, he forced his attention back to the spidery script.

And yet, the scuff of steps sounded very real. He whipped around to catch sight of a dark flutter between the trees.

"How do you spell that?" he demanded, giving silent thanks to the heavens there was no one around to see him shouting at shadows.

Hearing naught but the rustle of branches in reply, Rafael shook his head. His father had often told tales of Kent's mystical roots. Such childhood memories were provoking odd.

"D-E-C-"

He shot up from his seat, spilling the pencil and papers from his lap. "Who is there?" he called, taking a tentative step toward the forest. "A druid? A fairy?"

As if by magic, a figure materialized from among the tree trunks. "A very ordinary passer-by."

Rafael stared in openmouthed surprise. The hooded cloak and muslin gown were indeed unremarkable. But the young lady herself was a vision of ethereal beauty. Slim as a shaft of sunlight, with a delicate face pale as the morning mists. He blinked, half expecting the apparition to disappear in a puff of smoke.

She was still there, however, and eyeing him askance. "Shall I go on? Or have you decided you do not wish to write it down?"

He quickly retrieved his pencil and notebook.

Her voice still soft as the lakeside breeze, she spelled out the rest of the letters.

"Thank you." He looked up from the page, still unsure whether he was awake or dreaming. "As you have witnessed, my English leaves much to be desired."

"As does my Latin," she replied slowly. "*Theobroma cacao*? It sounds familiar and yet . . ."

"You know it as chocolate."

"Chocolate." Her expression was inscrutable, though he thought he saw a small spark of interest light in her eyes. They were, he noted, a deep leafy green, with flecks of gold that mirrored the cluster of curls framing her face. "That explains why I did not recognize it right away. I know most of the local flora by heart."

"Are you interested in plants?"

The young lady shrugged. She slanted a glance at the notes spread across the stone stab, but without further comment turned to the trees.

"Before you go, might I ask your help on one more word?" he asked quickly, loath for her to leave just yet.

She looked around.

"*Lanza*" he said in Spanish. "A shape of leaf, I think." He added, sketching a rough outline in the air. "Like so."

"Spear."

"Just so." Rafael scribbled it down in his notebook. "*Gracias, mea* lady," he said, the languages becoming hopelessly entangled in his head.

She hesitated, then ventured a question of her own. "Are you a botanist?"

"No, I am a . . ." He surveyed the scattered scribblings. "I am a fool, to think I could take on such a project. It would take a magician to turn all of this into a coherent book."

"A book on what?"

"Chocolate."

"Interesting." However, the arch of her brow added a touch of skepticism.

"Actually, it is," he replied. "My grandmother was quite an expert on the history and lore of the cacao tree. She spent a good part of her life collecting all manner of fascinating stories and tidbits." Grabbing a paper at random, he smoothed out the creases. "Here let me read you an example of ancient Aztec legend."

"Intriguing," she admitted, when he had finished the short passage. "However, might I make a suggestion for rewording the last sentence? As it is, it sounds a bit awkward."

He made a note of her corrections.

"Do you pass by here often?"

She shied back, a look of wariness clouding her gaze.

"That is," he added quickly. "I thought perhaps you might consent to hear some other chapters and offer your criticisms."

She shook her head.

"Can I tempt you to change your mind? The book will also include a mouthwatering selection of her recipes." Rafael added a smile, hoping to soften her solemn expression. "Dona Maria's true genius came to light in the kitchen. In her hands, chocolate lived up to its name as 'Food of the Gods.' You have never tasted anything so sublime as her breakfast blend of the beans. Fragrant vanilla, peppery chilies and cane sugar from the island of Barbados."

Her reaction was not at all what he expected.

A splash of color darkened her cheeks and her lips puckered. "I don't care for hot chocolate."

He could not quite believe his ears. A lady who didn't love chocolate? "What do you favor?"

"A sip of black tea. Or nothing at all. I'm not very hungry in the morning."

"*Madonna*," Rafael let out a low whistle. "No wonder you are thin as a wraith. My grandmother often spoke of how cacao is considered a medicine by many physicians who use it to nourish the ill and the infirm."

She gasped and spun around.

"Wait! I did not mean to imply—"

Too late. Like a flicker of quicksilver, she had already melted into the sun-dappled foliage.

"Damn." Pursuit was pointless. He would only end up hopelessly lost in the wooded moors.

He kicked at a pebble and watched it skitter across the terrace and fall into the water. In both Spanish and English, his linguistic skills seemed to be sunk beneath reproach. He had not only appeared a stuttering idiot, but a clumsy oaf to boot. After all, he had just put his foot in his mouth.

Dona Maria's notes on chocolate suddenly took on a bittersweet taste. Deciding he had done enough work for the day, Rafael fell to stuffing the papers into his satchel. After a last look at the forest, he slung it over his shoulder and set off on the long walk home.

KYRA HURRIED along the leafy path, but her thoughts lingered on the mysterious stranger.

A corsair. He reminded her of an engraving she had seen in a book on the Barbary pirates. *Dangerous.*

A shiver ran down her spine. Unlike the polished perfection of Lord Matherton, the stranger's features were rugged, scuffed by sun and wind. His olive skin added to his raffish look. As did his black hair, which fell in devil-may-care curls that grazed his shoulders. Chas affected a tumble of curls, too. But somehow the effect appeared artfully arranged, as if he had spent hours in front of the mirror.

And then there were the stranger's eyes, a deep ocean blue, their depths dark as midnight sin.

Sin. Kyra bit her lip. All men could go to the devil. She had learned her lesson about Spanish coin. Flatteries which lost their luster. Promises whose glitter proved false once they had bought what they wanted.

No, she would not be seduced into thinking the Spanish stranger was nice, simply because he had a sweet smile and self-deprecating sense of humor.

Nor would she think of chocolate, though the engravings she had seen of the cacao tree made it appear an appealing subject to paint. The fruit looked to have a variety of sizes and textures, with colors that ranged from ripe orange to lush purple. There was something exotic about it. *Enticing.*

Shaking off the wicked, wanton tingle in her fingertips, Kyra paused by a thicket of gorse and carefully clipped a sprig of the prickly blooms. She would stick to less fanciful flora. Sweet dreams, like dark-haired strangers, could only lead a young lady into trouble.

"Your wood sprite was most likely the Duke of Pierpont's daughter. A sad story, by all accounts." Hendrie shook his head. "Rumor has it Lady Kyra is no better than she should be."

Rafael could not quite puzzle out his uncle's meaning. "Sir?"

"A wayward lass."

"Wayward?" he repeated. "But she seemed quite sure of where she was headed."

A ghost of a smile fluttered on Hendrie's lips. "Forgive me, Rafael. Your English is so good, I sometimes forget you may not know the nuances of the language. In plain speaking, what I meant is that the young lady is said to have surrendered her virtue. 'Ruined' is yet another way of putting it. But, however it is said, the meaning is the same. She is now an outcast from Society, a shame to her family." The earl sighed as he swirled his brandy. "Pierpont must be devastated, with this tragedy following so closely on the heels of the other."

"What other tragedy, Uncle Aubrey?"

"The duke's younger daughter was killed in a riding accident.

A midnight race over dangerous ground, instigated by her sister over some trifling wager. Lady Kyra has always been known for her wildness."

Rafael saw the earl's expression shade with sorrow. "And yet, you speak as if you are fond of the young lady."

"I am." Hendrie stared rather wistfully into the fire. "Jack thought her a great gun. Said she had more spirit and courage than most lads. If I recall, there were several times when she outrode him in some rush to adventure. And outfoxed him as well, leaving him to take the blame for their mischief."

"She must be a clever lass to have bested Jack at his own game." Rafael, too, watched the flames lick up around the logs, feeling an odd sort of sadness for the young lady. A female who showed a spark of fire ended up getting burned, while a man was cast in a much different light.

"It seems unfair," he said slowly. "Jack enjoyed the favors of many a *signorita* in Spain, and was only thought the better for it by his peers. Yet a young lady gives way to a moment of passion, and she is ruined forever."

The earl looked shocked at such sentiment, then thoughtful. "It has always been thus."

"That does not make it right." Rafael frowned. No wonder she had shied away from his smiles. "After all, for the young lady to have erred, she must have had a partner. What is said of him in English Society?"

"Oh, he is definitely considered a cad," assured Hendrie. "But from what I hear, Lady Kyra refuses to name the fellow."

Steadfast loyalty, however undeserved, took courage, especially in the face of overwhelming odds. Rafael found himself liking her even more.

His uncle looked slightly abashed at being privy to gossip. "It is not that I seek out such scandalous talk. But my housekeeper's sister serves in the same position at Pierpont Hall, and Mrs. Ganton does like to chat during our morning meetings." He sipped at his brandy. "In truth, I pay little attention to the details of Lady Kyra's disgrace, but I am pleased to hear that she is recovering from her own injuries."

"She was hurt in the accident?"

"A broken leg, which is nearly healed. But as for her spirits, it seems she is a mere shadow of her former self. She barely eats or speaks, and spends most of her hours alone in her workroom, painting botanical watercolors. When she does venture outside her own quarters it is only to gather specimens for her paintings.

A sketch of an idea took form in Rafael's head. "Does Mrs. Ganton say what sort of subjects the lady favors?"

"Why, er, I believe she has mentioned wildflowers, though I wouldn't know a larkspur from a holly bush." Hendrie turned slightly, the light from the hearth accentuating the hollows under his cheekbones and the deep cut lines that gave his eyes a down-cast look, even when he essayed a smile. "Forgive the melancholy musings of an old man. At my age, it is so very sad to hear of the bloom fading from one so young, and so full of promise. But let us turn to a more encouraging subject."

He rose and gathered up several books from the reading stand. "I have found some very interesting volumes on the New World that may prove useful in your research."

A DASHING SOLDIER, decorated for bravery. Kyra thought about what her maid had told her that morning about the Earl of Hendrie's visitor. So, the handsome Spaniard was an even more romantic figure than a corsair. Still, she could not help thinking of him as a pirate, a dark and dangerous specter come to plunder her peace of mind.

"The devil take it!" Kyra steadied her wayward shears in time to keep from ruining the twist of honeysuckle. It did not matter in what shape or form her imagination saw him. He might as well be the Man in the Moon, for all the distance she meant to keep between them. She had already flown far too close to the sun. She would not risk being burned again.

A snap of twigs, sharp as the crackle of coals. Steps cut through the tall grass and a shadow fell across her blade. The steel turned cold to the touch.

Kyra turned.

Limned in the afternoon light, the Spaniard looked like Lucifer ablaze. *Why, oh why, did her body betray her resolve?* She must be truly wicked at heart to feel a devilish tingle from head to toe.

"Ah, *signorina*, I hoped I might run into you again." He inclined a bow. "I owe you an apology, more than one in fact. To begin with, I neglected to properly introduce myself. I am Rafael de Villafranca Greeley."

Rafael. What a sinuous sound. It wrapped around the tongue like silky smooth toffee.

"No doubt you thought me an errant gypsy, on the prowl for something to steal," he continued. "But in truth, I am quite harmless. I am visiting my uncle, the Earl of Hendrie."

"Yes, my maid made mention that His Lordship had a relative staying for a time."

"I think, perhaps, there is a connection between our two families. Are you perchance Lady Kyra Sterling?"

She nodded, searching his face for some sign of a smirk. What gossip had he heard?

His smile, however, seemed as sweet as the day before. "Please allow me to offer a formal acknowledgment of the acquaintance. I have heard that my cousin Jack considered you a good friend." His breath was whisper soft against her knuckles as he bent low over her hand. "And a formal apology for my awkward language. My English leaves much to be desired."

"On the contrary, sir. You speak very handsomely." Dear God, would he think she was encouraging a flirtation? She turned abruptly. "My condolences about Jack. He was indeed a dear friend, and I shall miss him. But unfortunately, I cannot tarry for a talk. These flowers will wilt without water." Grabbing up her basket of cuttings, she added a curt dismissal over her shoulder. "I am sure you will make great strides while you are here."

"As to that, *señorita* . . ." He fell in step beside her. "Might I ask you to read one other passage? It will only take a few moments, and the folly is close by."

Folly indeed. Kyra had every intention of saying no, but the word stuck in her throat.

"*Gracias.*" He had already tucked her hand in the crook of his elbow. "And today I come ready to repay your kindness in helping me with my English."

"You do not owe me anything, sir. Indeed, it is hardly worth mentioning a few trifling words."

"It is naught but a tiny token of thanks." He reached in his pocket and withdrew a small round object wrapped in a twist of marbled paper. The swirls of burnt amber and buttery yellow rolled to the center of his tanned palm.

Rafael de Villafranca Greeley looked to have a strong hand, thought Kyra. A capable hand, the hardened calluses complementing its long-fingered grace.

She tightened her grip on her basket of cuttings. "Still, I do not feel right in accepting it."

"Then we shall share it."

Even with its wrappings, the object looked no bigger than walnut. Curiosity got the better of her. "Pray, what is it?"

Rafael crossed to the far end of the folly before answering. "Open it and see." Before she could demur, he took her basket and set it down next to the portfolios on the stone slab.

The paper fell away to reveal a ball of rich brown paste flecked with bits of scarlet. Its soft sheen had the patina of oiled mahogany. Still mystified, she looked up.

"It is a special blend of cacao, made according to my grandmother's recipe," he explained. "Will you join me in a taste? It takes only a few minutes to prepare, and it will fortify our stamina for an attack on English grammar."

Surely he did not mean *now*. "But you have no kitchen, no cook."

"I have all the utensils I need right here." He produced a tin pot from his satchel, along with a small knife and two mugs. "As for a cook . . ." Wielding a wooden whisk, Rafael cut a rakish flourish though the air. "I have honed my skills under the tutelage of a culinary master."

"You!" Kyra could not contain her surprise. "Men don't cook."

"*Au contraire.*" His fingers moved with a fluid grace, assembling a pyramid of twigs and leaves in the crude stone hearth. "Only think of the best French chefs—are they not all male?"

A spark from flint striking steel lit the smile in his eyes. A leaf curled in the first flare of flame.

Kyra suddenly felt warm all over. "Yes, but English gentlemen—"

"Ah, but I am no English gentleman. I am afraid I share some of the same hot-blooded temperament as our Gallic enemy. Mayhap is it the Mediterranean sun that gives rise to a fervor for artistic expression." The whisk came to life between his palms, whipping the boiling water, shaved cacao and cane sugar to a creamy froth. "Like painting or music, cooking requires a passion for creativity."

Rafael pour out a measure of the brew and passed her a steaming mug. Their hands touched, and she was far more aware of the heat of his fingertips.

Was he flirting with her? If he knew the truth, he would have little taste for her company.

She colored and drew back, angry with the handsome Spaniard for stirring a longing that ought to have died. Angry with herself for feeling fire where there ought to be ice.

Having made up her mind to dislike the beverage, Kyra puckered her lips as she raised the mug, determined to abstain from more than a tiny swallow. But then she experienced the oddest sensation. The aroma of tropical fruit and roasted spice tickled her nose, the swirling sweetness filled her lungs and caressed her cheeks.

Dizzy, she smiled in spite of her resolve. A splash fell on her tongue, hot and heady. She drew in a mouthful and downed it in a quick gulp.

He looked at her from over the rim of his own mug. "It is good, isn't it?"

"Delicious," she said. "I shouldn't . . ."

"Why not? Chocolate is one of life's little pleasures."

Kyra froze. His smile was a reminder that life held little pleasure. Only pain and remorse.

He caught her wrist as she tried to flee. "Please, *signorina*. Has my faulty English once again led me to make some gaffe?"

"No, you said nothing wrong, sir." Guilt choked her words to a mere whisper. "It's just that I must go."

"First finish your chocolate. My grandmother believed it was bad luck to leave a drop in the cup."

"What would you know of bad luck?" Kyra fought back tears. "Gentlemen never have a difficulty in drinking their fill of sweet pleasures."

"Oh, I assure you that I, too, have experienced moments when life seems too bitter to swallow. When your heart is so empty that you feel not even an ocean of chocolate would fill the void. And yet, you must try, drop by drop. Otherwise, you will drown in despair."

Shame flooded her face. In her own self-absorbed struggle, she had momentarily forgotten about his cousin's recent death. "How selfish of me to imply no one else suffers from vagaries of Fortune. As I said, I am so very sorry about Jack. We shared a number of childhood adventures, and though we had seen little of each other over the past few years, I remember him as always having a smile on his face."

"Always." Rafael looked away to the lake. Through the fringe of dark lashes, his expression was unfathomable. "Even as he fell after taking the saber slash aimed at my head." He raised his mug.

A salute? She watched as sunlight danced around its rim.

It seemed unfair to let him drink alone. "To Jack."

The clink of cups broke his silence. "Yes, to Jack." He blinked. "Who was not afraid to look the devil in the eye and laugh."

The steam of the chocolate must have misted his gaze. How else to explain the beads of moisture beneath his eyes.

"I hear his laugh often, you know."

Kyra nodded. "Like an echo of . . . loss."

"For our loved ones as well as our innocence." He lifted the chocolate to his lips. "My grandmother was very fond of a toast she learned from her Jewish friends. *Laichayam.* It means 'To life.' She heartily approved of the fact that food and drink are an integral part of such sentiment."

"She sounds like a remarkable lady." Kyra joined him in savoring the last piquant taste of the contessa's special blend.

"She was." Rafael smiled, but his voice betrayed a pinch of sadness. Kyra sensed that the loss was more than a distant memory from the past. He sat on the edge of the bench, his hands smoothing at the dog-eared notebooks spread across the stone. "I miss her. But in leaving the legacy of her notes and recipes, I shall always have a small part of Dona Maria with me."

Though his words stirred a great many questions, Kyra was too shy to ask him for any details. Neither of them spoke for some time, but strangely enough, it was a companionable silence, soothing as the gentle lapping of the lake and last little swirl of chocolate at the bottom of her mug.

She made sure that not a drop was left before she set it aside. "Thank you for sharing your chocolate, sir. It was . . ."

"Unusual? Unexpected? Unique?"

"It seems you have no need for help with English vocabulary.

"But like the ingredients for cacao balls of the Paria peninsula, if they are not combined correctly, the results will be disastrous." He made a wry face. "However, I shall just have to improvise as I go along."

"If you still wish for me to read your chapter, I suppose I could spare a little time tomorrow." As Kyra stole a look at the piles of paper, she could not help but add, "Cacao balls of the Paria peninsula? Surely that is a recipe of your own whimsy. I mean, chocolate is chocolate. How many different way may a beverage be served?"

"I think you may be surprised by just how many forms the magic of *Theobroma cacao* can take."

Surely he was just exaggerating, she thought as she rose and took up her basket. But just one was more than enough. Surprisingly, she did feel better, though it was hard to describe how.

It was as if the gaping hole in her heart had shrunk just a tiny bit.

Drawing in a breath, she shook off the thought. That would surely be magic. And magic happened only in fairy tales, not in real life.

CHAPTER 4

Rafael swirled his glass and watched the flicker of the candle flames set off sparks of amber-gold in the tawny port. The exact same shade of Lady Kyra's hair when it shimmered in the sunlight, he mused, though as far as he could see, the young lady lingered far too much in the shadows.

"You seem pensive." His uncle looked up from the book he was reading. "I hope you are not growing too bored here in the country."

"Not at all," he replied. "Your hospitality—"

"I would like to think we can progress beyond polite platitudes, Rafael." Hendrie fixed him with a fond smile. "We are family, and more than that, you are now my heir. I hope we can develop a degree of friendship and honesty between each other."

"Nothing would please me more," he replied softly. "I did not mean to seem distant. It is just that . . ." He drew in a ragged breath. "That it is very complicated."

"It is, indeed. But then, life is never simple, even in the best of circumstances."

The reply encouraged him to be frank. "To be truthful, I feel so very strange usurping Jack's place."

"You mustn't think of it like that. I don't." Hendrie rose and went to the sideboard to pour himself a glass of wine. "Jack's place will always be here, unaltered." He touched a hand to his heart. "If you will join him there, it would be a joy to me and a light to help counter the darkness."

"I would be truly honored, Uncle Aubrey."

"As would I." He lifted his glass. "Come let us drink a cheerful toast, rather than a maudlin one. Your mother, my sister by marriage, loved sharing laughter when we were young. I hope we shall come to do the same."

"To laughter," agreed Rafael. *May light and laughter brighten both this house and our hearts.*

"I should like to hear more about the battle, and Jack's last moments, if it would not cause you too much pain," asked Hendrie, once they had both savored a swallow of the wine. "Both you and the general have given me the facts, but . . ." He let his gaze drop down to the glass clasped in his frail hands. "Does it seem terribly macabre that I wish to have a better picture in my mind's eye of his final hours?"

Rafael felt a clench of guilt. He should have realized his uncle would want more than token words of heroism to hold as precious memories. "It is not macabre at all. It's just that I wasn't sure how to."

"No apologies, Rafael," interrupted Hendrie gently. "You have nothing for which to be sorry."

He drew in a steadying breath. "It was a brutally hot day. The dust was choking, and the sun beat down relentlessly, its rays burning like fire against the flesh. Our infantry units were outnumbered, and despite their tenacious fighting, the French were slowly forcing them back. The losses on both sides were staggering." He paused, feeling his throat grow dry. "General Graham knew it was imperative to hold the pass for Wellington's forces. So, despite the odds against us, he ordered our cavalry regiment to charge and try to regain the high ground on the left flank, so that we might position our artillery there and turn the tide."

Hendrie nodded for him to go on.

"The French send their elite Hussars to counter our charge. The clash was fierce beyond description." There were many nights when Rafael awoke in a cold sweat with the ring of steel reverberating in his ears. "My horse was killed by a pistol shot and I fell, entangled in the stirrups, amid a welter of slashing hooves. A French officer swung his saber, cutting my leg. I was helpless, for my weapon was pinned beneath my mount, and as I saw the saber rise again, I knew it was aimed at my heart."

He managed another breath, though his chest felt as if a vise of iron was clamped around his chest. "Suddenly, Jack appeared, and spurred his stallion forward. He swung his own saber, but his horse stumbled and the blow missed. The Frenchman twisted and his blade caught Jack square in the chest. Our eyes met for an instant and then he fell back, and I passed out."

"Thank you," said Hendrie after a long moment. "It is a great comfort to know the details. And a great comfort to know that Jack died as he would have wished." A small smile tugged at his uncle's mouth. "You held the pass that day, which was crucial to Wellington's advance. Jack would have considered that worth his life."

"General Graham sent our troops to search for his body during the truce that followed the fighting." A time for tending to the wounded and dead was usual after any battle. "But the French had already sent their burial parties to the hillside. Our men found Jack's saber, but they were assured that all British casualties were buried with full honors." said Rafael.

"Thank you," repeated his uncle. "I know how hard it was for you to be forced to relive those awful moments."

Coals crackled in the hearth as flames flared up from the burning logs.

"And now, let us put the past aside and look to the future."

Hendrie took a small sip of his port and then quickly changed the subject. "Is your work progressing well?"

"Yes, in fact it is." Despite the difficulty of talking about the terrible day, Rafael sensed that both he and his uncle felt as if a weight had been lifted from their shoulders. "I hadn't quite expected to be so captivated by the subject, but Dona Maria makes the subject come alive."

He suddenly thought about their wraith-like neighbor and sight of her slender form flitting through the woods and fields. "She makes *Theobroma cacao* so much more than a mere academic interest. Through her eyes, I see the magic of its essence." He pursed his lips. "Though I daresay that sounds exceedingly odd to you."

"Not at all," said his uncle softly. "There is much magic in the world around us if we would let ourselves be open to seeing it."

Rafael was once again very glad he had made the journey to England.

A chuckle made him look up from his glass. "Speaking of magic, Cook has mentioned your activities in the kitchen. It seems you are brewing up a bit of magic as well as writing about it."

"I do hope it is not causing any problems."

"No, no, not at all! It is unusual for a gentleman to have any interest in culinary concerns, but she is intrigued by your endeavors, and very curious. Apparently the sweet scents have everyone dying to know what you are up to."

Rafael grinned. "I shall be happy to present them with a platter of bonbons from my next batch. And perhaps you would like to try a new spiced version of hot chocolate for your breakfast drink."

"I am very fond of my morning coffee," answered Hendrie. "But I should like very much to taste any new concoctions you create."

"We will soon have to send to London for more supplies. I'm

afraid the local purveyors don't carry many of the ingredients I need, and I seem to be running out of items more quickly than I anticipated."

"I am delighted to aid in your research. Leave a list with Cook and we'll send it off tomorrow."

Rafael was already composing a mental list of piquant spices and pungent tropical sugars that he wished to share with Lady Kyra. "You know, I have heard that the Covent Garden markets offer quite an interesting mix of exotic items. And it has been a long time since I've visited London. So perhaps I shall go up to Town and see for myself. If I leave very early in the morning, I should be able to be back by evening."

"An excellent idea. The hustle and bustle of the city will make for a nice change from the quiet of Hendrie Hall. Just let John Coachman know when you wish to make the journey and he will have the carriage ready."

KYRA PUT down her brush and stepped back to assess her painting. *Not bad, considering she was merely copying from an old engraving.* But the textures and colors shown in the old volume of botanical prints made her long to see some actual examples of *Theobroma cacao.* The nuances looked infinitely intriguing—like the surprising flavors of Rafael de Villafranca Greeley's frothy hot chocolate drink.

Like the subtle range of hues in his sea-blue eyes.

She quickly looked away from her palette, quashing the urge to sketch a portrait of the Spaniard's handsome face. Plants—it was much safer to stay with plants. Their beauty was benign and didn't cause heartache or pain.

What about foxglove or stinging nettles? piped up a small voice in her head. *There is both good and evil in all of Nature.*

As she carefully rinsed her brushes, she couldn't help thinking about the idea. *Good and Evil.* Was it possible that in allowing darkness to overshadow all of the light in her life she was letting evil have the ultimate triumph over her?

Kyra felt a frown furrow her brow. There would be no easy answers to such a complex, confusing question. Just the thought of trying to contemplate it was a little daunting and frightening.

But perhaps it was time to stop being afraid of her own shadow.

Still in a pensive frame of mind, she left her workroom and wandered down the corridor to the library. There were several more books on tropical plants and she gathered them up, along with a book of maps on the Caribbean islands. As she turned, the scent of tobacco smoke wafted into the alcove.

"That is quite a pile. Here, please let me help you carry them back to your workroom."

Kyra allowed her father to take half the pile from her arms.

His brows rose on reading over the titles, but he made no comment save to say, "I will be going up to Town on the morrow. Are there any books or art supplies you wish to have brought back?"

"I am running low on several shades of watercolor pigment, so a fresh batch from Watman's Emporium would be very welcome," she said.

"Just write out a list and I shall see that Jenkins purchases them."

"Thank you, Papa." Kyra hesitated as they turned the corner of the corridor. *Dare she ask?* Before she could think twice about the decision, she let the words slip free. "I was wondering. Might I come along? I was thinking that my maid and I might spend a few hours exploring Kew Gardens while you are taking care of your affairs in the city."

The low flame of the wall sconce caught the flicker of light that lit in the duke's iron-gray eyes. "By Jove, I think that a splendid idea!" he exclaimed. "I seem to recall reading in the newspaper that they have recently received a new shipment of tropical specimen plantings from the West Indies."

"Yes, and it's said to include some very rare flowers," she replied. "I thought I would bring along my sketchbook and do some quick studies. It is always inspiring to try a new subject."

"Excellent, excellent!" he exclaimed, his face wreathing in a smile. "Let us leave bright and early, so you have plenty of time to stroll through the pathways and conservatories."

"Thank you," she repeated, feeling a pinch of guilt at how the timid request had sparked such a look of hope. It reminded her again of how her actions had hurt the ones she loved. For an instant, she was tempted to retreat, to make up a cowardly excuse to put off the trip.

But she couldn't bear to disappoint him yet again. "Good night, Papa. I had best retire if we are to rise at the crack of dawn."

THE NEXT MORNING, as the carriage drew closer to the city, Kyra was feeling even more unsettled about her decision. Living in her own isolated little enclave, she had forgotten just how noisy and crowded the main thoroughfare could be—carriages jostled with the farm carts and brewery wagons, drovers called curses at the young bucks racing their curricles at a reckless pace.

A part of her cringed at all the commotion and yet, a part of her felt the thrum of activity stir a certain frisson of excitement. Clenching her hands in her lap, she tried to still her quickening pulse. This wasn't her world anymore, and never would be. She was an outcast.

"We are almost there." Her father shifted to glance out the window, drawing her out of her own mordant thoughts. "You have an extra shawl in case it turns chilly?"

"Yes, Papa."

Turning to her maid, who was busy arranging the parcels piled on the seat beside her, the duke asked. "And you have the picnic that Cook prepared?"

"Yes, Your Grace." The young woman indicated the hamper, which looked to have enough food to feed a regiment. "And a blanket in case the ground is a trifle damp."

He pulled out his pocket watch and blew out his cheeks. "Well, then. I shall leave William with you to carry the parcels. We shall return around two if that suits you."

"Please do not feel that you need to rush through your errands on account of me." Already Kyra could see a hint of intriguing colors poking up from flowerbeds bordering the nearby walkways. "There is so much to see here."

"You can always come back another day."

Much as her fingers itched to take up her brushes and water-colors, she felt butterflies begin to flutter in her stomach for a moment as the carriage door opened and the iron steps were set down. But on seeing a pinch of concern thin her father's mouth, she made herself descend.

There was nothing to be nervous about, she chided to herself. None of her acquaintances from Town visited places like this. They spent their time within the gilded splendor of the grand mansions in Mayfair, gossiping during the long hours of morning calls and then dancing until dawn at the fancy balls.

Strangely enough, she didn't really miss those things.

"Watch your step, milady, there are several puddles just ahead." Her maid, Anna, reached out to tuck the trailing fringe of Kyra's shawl around her shoulder.

"And mind the chill," added the footman as he caught up to them. "The breeze looks to be freshening."

She paused in the lee of two tall Lebanon cypress trees. "I appreciate your concern, but truly, I'm not quite the wilting flower that I appear."

They both looked a little abashed.

"Why don't the two of you pick out a nice spot for the picnic and arrange all our things, while I make some sketches."

"But I promised your father."

"I won't wander far," she assured. Seeing Anna's uncertainty, she added softly, "I appreciate your concern, but you know I prefer to work in solitude, and having the two of you hovering will be a distraction."

"Very well, milady." Her maid blew out a sigh that surrendered to a smile. "You go ahead and enjoy yourself. We'll follow along at a distance. But you have only to signal if you need us."

"Yes, of course." Kyra felt a flush of excitement warm her cheeks. For just a few precious hours, she would give herself the freedom to forget about the past and simply explore the present.

The pathways beckoned with all sorts of tantalizing botanical treasures, but as she took her small satchel of painting supplies from the footman, she knew exactly which specimens she wished to find. A quick question to one of the attendants directed her down a graveled walkway that led toward the Chinese pagoda. Tucked behind a high hedge of Sumatran yew, halfway down the sloping lawns, was a charming glass-paned conservatory.

After opening the door, Kyra stepped inside and was immediately enveloped in warm, moist air, redolent with the sweetly spiced scent of . . .

"Chocolate," she whispered to herself, breathing deeply and savoring the heady fragrance.

The colors, ranging from rich coppery oranges to pale lemony yellows, were also a feast for the senses. She stood for a bit, simply admiring the profusion of pods growing out from the slender trunks of the small trees. According to the brass plaques placed in the earthen beds, there were three species of *Theobroma cacao* on display—*criolla*, *forastera* and *trinitario*.

After one last deep inhale, Kyra set to work unwrapping her sketchbook, water jar and paintbox. Taking a seat on the teak bench set by the stone fountain, she mixed up the first batch of hues, touched her brush to the palette and turned to a blank page. So lost was she in her art that she wasn't aware of someone else entering the conservatory until a shadow fell across the paper.

"Oh!" She looked up with a start.

"Forgive me for startling you." Rafael flashed a tentative smile. "I was trying not to disturb you, but couldn't resist trying to steal a peek at your paintings."

"They are just rough sketches," Kyra replied, trying not to let her gaze linger on the sinuous curl of his lips. She quickly shut her book. "If I am lucky, there will be enough details for me to work up a finished piece."

"I have a feeling luck has nothing to do with it," he said. "Might I be allowed a closer look?"

Kyra hesitated.

"I beg your pardon." His expression squeezed to a wry grimace. "I have no doubt made some terribly rude request. I may be half English, but I seem to be wholly ignorant of the many complex rules of Polite Society."

A gentleman who could poke fun at himself? His self-deprecating humor was even more attractive than his smile. "Your manners are faultless, sir. Rather it is my own unpolished skills that hold me back. My art is simply for my own enjoyment."

"I assure you, I would enjoy it too, especially as the subject is one that is near and dear to my heart." He held out his hand. "Please?"

Had he made some flowery request, full of fulsome flatteries, she would have resisted. But it was impossible to deny his simple, straightforward appeal.

With a wordless nod, Kyra passed it over.

❧

UP CLOSE, the sketches were even more exquisite than he had guessed from the quick glance he had gotten before she had shut her book. There was a grace and fluidity to her brushstrokes that captured the living, growing essence of the cacao trees. And her eye for color was wonderfully nuanced. The subtle shadings of the elongated pods were beautifully rendered.

"These are quite marvelous," Rafael said as he carefully turned back through the pages for second look. "You have a rare talent."

A slight blush suffused her cheeks, a lovely shade of pale pink, softer and more delicate than a velvety rose petal. "You are too kind, milord."

Milord. The fact that, as heir to the earldom, he now bore Jack's courtesy title made him wince inwardly. However, he hid his reaction and replied, "My words are not flummeries, Lady Kyra, they are naught but the plain truth."

Her color deepened.

Seeing that he was embarrassing her, Rafael quickly shifted the conversation back to a more general discussion of art. Having some knowledge in the subject, he said, "What is your opinion of the botanical illustrations of Pierre-Joseph Redouté?"

"They are quite lovely," replied Kyra. "But for true genius I prefer the art of Maria Sibylla Merian."

"A lady artist?" he mused.

"Yes."

"I am not familiar with her work."

Kyra's chin rose a fraction. "That's hardly surprising. Females have a deucedly difficult time getting any recognition for their talents."

"They do," he agreed. "Which is most unfair."

His sentiments seemed to shock her. "You truly think so?" she asked warily.

"My grandmother was passionate about healing and had more knowledge in the field than any man I ever met. But her desire to study medicine at a university was met with derision in Spain. A lady, she was told, had not the intellect or the emotional stability to understand such advanced lessons." He let out a low snort. "As if men, by virtue of their plumbing, have been gifted with some great cerebral advantage."

Her eyes widened, and then a burble of laughter welled up in her throat. "Plain speaking indeed, sir!"

He gave a rueful lift of his shoulders. "I fear that I have offended you."

"Not at all," she assured him. "It's just that you are different."

Different. He wasn't sure if that was good or bad. But the fact that he had brought a laugh to her lips was gratifying. "I have a feeling that I have been, how do your English say it, damned with faint praise."

Kyra lowered her gaze. "If anyone is damned, it is me." She turned suddenly, the poke of her bonnet hiding her eyes. The movement set off a slight ruffling of the leaves, the play of shadows created by the sunlight slanting in through the mullioned glass further obscuring her expression.

"The colors of the pods are truly lovely, aren't they?" she said with what sounded like forced brightness. "Have you ever seen a live tree before?"

Much as he wished to reassure her that a mistake, however terrible the consequences, did not damn anyone to perdition, Rafael was uncertain whether his words would be welcome. He was, after all, a stranger, and a foreign one at that. So instead, he followed her lead in returning to a safer subject.

"Yes, my grandmother had a number of specimen plantings in her hacienda conservatory. She favored the *criolla* variety because it is the king of cacao—the most delicate, and difficult to grow, but the beans yield the most flavorful chocolate."

"Ah." She seemed to be studying every detail of the small *criolla* tree, as if committing them to memory. "I take it the beans are inside the pod?"

"They are. And it is a long and laborious process to turn them into the flavorful essence we call chocolate."

Kyra slanted him a sidelong look, and he gave an inward

smile, glad to see he had piqued her curiosity. "Indeed? I confess, I have no idea how it is done."

"When the pod is ripe, it's cut open and the beans can be found nestled in a milky substance." Rafael proceeded to explain the drying and grinding required to turn cacao into what the ancient Aztecs called 'the nectar of the Gods.'

As he spoke, Kyra listened intently, occasionally leaning closer to the specimen planting to examine a detail of the plants. "Fascinating," she said when he had finished.

"Even more fascinating is all the lore and legends that surround chocolate. My grandmother collected a host of historical facts and stories." He pursed his lips. "Though I am having a devil of a struggle trying to turn them into proper English."

Would she bite?

"If it would help, I could read over your pages from time to time. I have no knowledge of Spanish, but—"

"But that is not important at all," he assured her. "What matters is that it makes sense in English."

"Well, I do have a modicum of skill in that language."

Rafael couldn't help but notice that a smile, even a very faint one, transformed her whole face. The knife-edged cheekbones and the shadows beneath her eyes softened, and the paleness of her skin seemed to warm with a sun-kissed glow.

"*Bueno!* Then it is decided."

She opened her mouth to speak.

"I can't express how very grateful I am for your offer," he went on quickly. "It is a labor of love for me to see my grandmother's work published, so that others may share in her knowledge and wisdom. She believed very deeply in the potent healing powers of chocolate."

Kyra exhaled a long breath. "Well then, I shall be happy to help you. The idea is a noble one, but to be truthful, I don't believe in magical elixirs."

"What say you to both of us keeping an open mind on the subject?"

"Very well." She reached out and plucked her sketchbook from his grasp. "Just as long as you won't be disappointed when my thinking doesn't change."

We shall see, señorita, Rafael thought to himself. *We shall see.* He had long ago learned never to underestimate Dona Maria's extraordinary powers.

CHAPTER 5

"I should allow you to go back to your sketching." Giving an apologetic shrug, Rafael stepped back. "I fear I prosed on too long about the making of cacao when you would have much rather been engaged in your art."

"I enjoyed hearing it," said Kyra. "Having a better understanding about a plant helps me see it more clearly." She ducked her head. "Though I daresay that likely strikes you as silly."

"Not at all," he answered earnestly. "I think I know exactly what you mean."

Strangely enough, she believed he did. A soldier with a sensitive soul? It seemed a contradiction. Which made him a conundrum.

Puzzles, puzzles. But piecing together all the nuanced facets that made up Rafael de Villafranca Greeley was *not* a task that ought to occupy her imagination. He might as well be the Man in the Moon, a far-far away orb made of Stilton cheese, for how out of reach he was. To dream any differently was madness.

Keeping her gaze averted, Kyra began putting away her paints. "I ought to go as well. I promised my maid I would not be gone too long."

"Please allow me to escort you to where she is waiting."

Telling herself it would be churlish to refuse, she let him take her satchel. But deep down inside, she knew the real reason. His company made her forget for a moment her flaws and her fears.

"Are there other exotic plants you are looking forward to seeing here?" asked Rafael as he clicked open the glass door and led her back to the graveled walkway.

"Bougainvillea," she answered without hesitation. "The papery flower petals sound so intriguing."

He nodded thoughtfully. "I think you would like them. They create very interesting shapes and textures. And the colors, especially the deep pinks, can be very vivid. We had several specimens at our hacienda in Spain that were brought back from Mexico by a friend of my father."

"Was he interested in botany?"

"No, but he knew it would please my grandmother, so he made a habit of asking anyone he knew was traveling to the New World to bring back some tropical treasure for her collection."

"How very thoughtful_" A swirl of silk suddenly rounded the yew hedge up ahead, and as it materialized into three ladies, she felt her breath catch in her throat.

Oh, Lord, she should have known it was a mistake to leave the sanctuary of her father's estate.

For an instant, she was tempted to turn and flee, but it was already too late. The trio—a marchioness expensively dressed in the first crack of fashion and her two equally elegant daughters— were fast approaching.

Oh, if only the earth would open up beneath her feet and let her fall all the way to Cathay.

The all-too-familiar haughty stare of Lady Leverett swept right over her without a flicker of acknowledgment as she fixed Rafael with a brilliant smile. "Why, Lord Leete, how lovely to see you again."

Kyra saw him flinch at the marchioness's use of his late

cousin's title. It must have been a painful reminder of his loss. Nevertheless, he bowed politely.

"His Lordship and I met very briefly in Southampton, at the military reception your father hosted for Lord Stratton's returning regiment," she said to her companions. Turning back to him, she smoothed the stylish ribbons trimming her bonnet. "My husband, the Marquess of Leverett, has told us all about your heroics on the Peninsula, and my daughters are simply in alt to meet you. Please allow me to introduce you to Lady Caroline and Lady Margaret."

Still not a word or look was directed at her, noted Kyra. She might as well have been one of the ancient stone statues grouped by the yew hedge for all the attention the trio paid her.

Try as she might, she couldn't help but feel a flush begin to creep to her face. Caroline and Margaret had been part of her circle of friends. They had shared laughter and girlish confidences, which made the snub that much more hurtful.

Rafael hesitated, then pointedly said, "And allow me to introduce Lady Kyra—"

"We are acquainted," sniffed Lady Leverett. A frosty glance barely acknowledged Kyra.

His expression tightened.

"Since you are in London, sir, I do hope you will attend our soiree tonight," went on Lady Leverett. "I know all of Society is very eager to meet the new heir to the Hendrie earldom."

"Actually, I am simply visiting the city for the day. After my visit here, I will be returning to Hendrie Hall," he replied.

"What a pity. When might you be returning? I would love to hold a ball in your honor."

"At present, I have no plans to return to Town anytime soon. I am quite content to spend my time at my uncle's estate."

The marchioness looked a little taken aback. "Naturally you will wish to acquaint yourself with its running, as you are now the heir."

Kyra watched another shadow of emotion ripple through his eyes. *Was Lady Leverett oblivious to her tactless words?* But of course she was. He was a handsome, eligible bachelor—a rich and titled bachelor—and the marchioness had two daughters to marry off.

"But the quiet of the country will no doubt become rather boring, so you must come enjoy the gaiety of Town life too," continued Lady Leverett as she shot a coy look at her daughters. "All young men take pleasure in the festive swirl of Society and the company of the young ladies."

Out of the corner of her eye, Kyra saw that Rafael did not crack a smile. Indeed, his expression had lost any hint of humor, and his blue eyes had darkened to a stormy hue. "Actually, the quiet of the country suits me very well." He touched a hand to the brim of his curly beaver hat. "And now, if you will excuse us, I must escort Lady Kyra back to her maid."

The marchioness exhaled sharply, her nostrils flaring in irritation.

"Good day, ladies," added Rafael, inclining a small nod to her daughters. He then curled his gloved hand around Kyra's elbow and guided her forward.

She kept her spine straight, even though she heard the huffing and whispers behind her back.

"Are all English aristocrats so unconscionably rude?" he muttered once they were out of earshot.

She clenched her teeth, too embarrassed to answer. Spotting Anna and William at the crest of the hill, she tried to quicken her steps, anxious to escape . . . though no matter how fast she might run, she could never outpace her shame. It would always be there, clinging to her skirts like a shadow for the rest of her days.

However, his grip tightened, holding her back.

"Lady Kyra—"

The sting of tears prickled against the back of her lids. "Please, I am late and I must hurry," she said in a rush.

"Another few minutes will make no difference," he said gently. "I don't understand."

"Milord." It hadn't occurred to her to call him by Jack's title and she couldn't quite bring herself to do so now. "You have no need to trouble yourself about it. Truly, it is no concern to you. And I would prefer not to talk about it."

"But it *does* concern me," he replied. "Those ladies were unkind to you."

As they rounded the tall hedge, Kyra came to a halt. Her throat felt too tight for words, yet she forced herself to speak. "Surely my uncle has explained why."

Rafael's mouth pinched in at the corners. "He has mentioned your accident."

"You are being tactful, sir. But I am sure he has also mentioned my ruined reputation." She hugged her arms to her chest and tried to keep her voice from sounding too brittle. "The truth is, I am considered an outcast, a blot on the family's honor. As you saw, I am shunned by Polite Society." She blinked, refusing to seem even more pitiable by letting the tears pearled on her lashes spill down her cheeks. "I should have known better than to come here. To venture out in public is to invite scenes like you just witnessed."

He stood silent, his gaze downcast so it was impossible to see his eyes through the thick fringe of his dark lashes.

"It would be best if you avoid me from now on," she went on. "I should not wish for my own black deeds to somehow rub off on you and sully your introduction to the *ton*.

"If Lady Leverett and her daughters are any example of the cruel and callous people who call themselves the flower of English nobility, then I have absolutely no interest in becoming part of their world."

"You don't understand, sir," she exclaimed, unconsciously echoing his words. "To be cut off from Society is to be isolated, to be . . ."

How to describe the feeling of utter loneliness? She deserved it, but he most certainly didn't.

"To be alone?" He crooked a smile. "I don't need a ballroom full of pompous popinjays flapping around me to feel comfortable. I am very happy with just myself for company, or better yet, a circle of people whose hearts and minds I can respect."

Respect?

She swallowed hard, but before she could respond, her maid cut across the lawn, a bit breathless from hurrying down the hill. "I beg your pardon, milady, but your father's carriage is approaching." She bobbed an apologetic curtsey to Rafael. "Please come have a quick bit of sustenance before George packs up the picnic—you haven't eaten since breakfast."

"Thank you, Anna, but I would rather not delay our return home." Kyra glanced up at the dark clouds scudding in from the west. "Besides, I'm not really hungry."

Her maid clucked in concern as Rafael pulled his handkerchief from his pocket and unwrapped it to reveal several glossy nut-brown disks. "Take these for the journey."

Seeing her look of puzzlement, he broke off a small piece. "I shall explain. But first, open your mouth."

"Wha—"

He placed the morsel on her tongue.

A meltingly sweet essence tickled at her senses. *Sugar, spice, the crunch of nutmeats, the smooth richness of vanilla . . .*

Kyra chewed slowly, savoring all the flavors. "Oh, that's divine." She swallowed. "It tastes like chocolate, but how can that be? Chocolate is a beverage, not a food."

"Edible chocolate has been in existence for centuries," he corrected. "The Ancient Aztecs made it into wafers for their warriors, who consumed it for strength and endurance during their long marches and battles."

"It tastes too good to be medicinal," she quipped.

"Medicine can come in many guises." Rafael handed her the

rest of the confections. "The art of edible chocolate was more recently perfected by a Frenchman named Sulpice Debauve. He was pharmacist to King Louis XVI and Marie Antoinette. When the queen complained about the taste of her medicines, he concocted chocolate *pistoles* such as these to disguise it. Her favorite flavor was said to be almond milk."

She broke off another bite. "You know such fascinating stories."

"Chocolate is an endlessly fascinating subject."

"Lady Kyra," murmured her maid.

"Yes, yes, I am coming." She polished off the rest of the *pistole* and put the others in the pocket of her pelisse. "I feel well fortified for the journey, though I am glad not to be tackling tropical jungles or towering mountains."

"We shall soon have you ready to conquer any obstacle, Lady Kyra," said Rafael softly.

"Let us not go that far. But thank you." She took back her satchel. "For everything, sir."

"That's a nice gentleman, if you don't mind me saying so," Anna said, as they made their way up to where George was waiting with the hamper and blankets. "He seems ever so kind and considerate."

"Yes," mused Kyra. "He is very nice."

The trouble was, she didn't know whether that made her want to smile or sob.

RAFAEL CLIMBED down from his carriage, but despite the mizzling rain and chill mists teasing at the upturned collar of his coat, he was in no hurry to return to the manor house. Instead, he chose walk along the bridle path leading up to the high meadow overlooking the lake. On the other side of the water, the valley stretched off to the faraway hills, their fuzzed shapes deepening to shades of purple and indigo in the fading light. The Duke of Pierpont's lands lay to the left of the thick stand of ancient oaks. Over the lofty treetops, he could just make out the boundary walls of mossy stone edging the wheat fields.

Was Kyra home by now? Was she eating more than a sparrow-like peck of nourishment?

Damn the cowardly cur who had brought such a look of sadness to her luminous green eyes. Not for the first time, he found himself reflecting on the unfairness of the rules governing men and women.

"Lord knows, I have no claims to being a saint," he muttered. During the years he had spent fighting in Portugal and Spain, there had been several *senoras* who had shared his bed, but for a man, such dalliances only earned the respect of his peers, not their revulsion.

"I am lauded for my seduction skills." His partners were never innocents, of course, but worldly widows or women whose marriages were naught but matches of convenience. They were experienced enough to know how to play the game without suffering any consequences. "But seduction," he whispered, "is a two-edged sword for females."

Rafael blew out a gusty sigh. When an innocent young lady succumbed to the charms of a gentleman, Society considered her ruined for life.

One mistake.

His hands tightened on the reins as he thought about her erstwhile fiancé, who had callously abandoned her when rumors began to fly. He knew little about their courtship, or the events that led to the terrible tragedy of that fateful night's horse race. But he couldn't shake the feeling that there was something havey-cavey about the matter.

He shifted in his saddle as the shadows lengthened over the landscape, long-fingered shapes that seemed to squeeze the light from the surroundings.

But why, he wondered, was he taking the matter so much to heart? There was an old English adage that his mother had often repeated to him when he was a child. *Whatever bed you make, you must sleep in it.* He barely knew Lady Kyra Sterling.

But Jack had.

The memories had come back slowly, perhaps because a shroud of pain still clouded his mind when he tried to think about his cousin. Yet he had forced himself to recall the good times, the laughter and the bonds of friendship, as well as those last awful moments in the heat of battle. And that was when the realization struck him.

Kyra had written regularly to Jack, and her thoughtful letters, filled with funny anecdotes about home, and light-hearted accounts of the friends and parties in Town, had been a source of immeasurable cheer for his cousin. She had teased him too, bringing laughter to his lips as he sat around a campfire, far, far from home.

Jack had shared her letters with him, along with stories of their youthful escapades together. It was clear that he loved her, not romantically, but as a sister. And he would not have stood back and let her be destroyed by ugly rumors and innuendo. Whatever the truth, Jack would have remained a loyal friend and fought to have her forgiven.

There were ways to influence the *ton*. Her father was a duke, a powerful and respected member of Society. And Jack was extremely popular among his peers. With his support, Kyra would have had a fighting chance for redemption.

But Jack wasn't here . . .

"And so it is up to me to take his place," said Rafael. Lifting his eyes to the rain-dark sky, he swore a silent promise to do all he could to aid the young lady in mending her shredded reputation.

But first, he would have to convince her that she was not beyond help.

And that, he thought wryly, would be no easy task.

CHAPTER 6

The butler gave a discreet cough as he paused by the open doorway of Kyra's workroom. "You have a visitor, milady."

Surprised, she turned from her easel.

Who would visit?

"Forgive me for intruding, Lady Kyra." Rafael moved to stand alongside Gorman. "It was such a fine day, I decided to take a walk from the folly, and the path led to here. So, I thought I would stop in to pay my regards, but only if I am not intruding on your work. I would not want you to start thinking of me as an unwelcome distraction."

A distraction. The handsome Spaniard was certainly that, and though she should—*she must*—consider him an unwelcome one, she couldn't help but feel a flutter of happiness.

"You are never intruding, sir." Kyra set aside her brush. "You must be tired and thirsty after such a long trek." To the butler she added, "Gorman, kindly have tea and cakes brought to the west parlor."

"Yes, milady."

"Please follow me," she said, joining Rafael in the corridor and then leading the way to an airy, sun-filled room with glass-paned doors overlooking the back gardens. Draperies made of floral chintz framed the tall windows, the soft colors reflected in the pastel upholstery of the furniture. The effect created a feeling of buttery warmth.

"What a pleasant place," he remarked, after pausing to admire a set of hand-colored botanical engravings of roses.

"Yes, it is especially nice in the afternoon." Kyra took a seat on the sofa and gestured for him to join her. "Your leg looks to be getting stronger," she said as he settled himself on the cushions.

"The doctors advised daily exercise, and walking does seem to be helping." He glanced at her skirts. "You, too, seem to be making great strides in recovering."

"I suppose so." In truth, she felt a little guilty that her limp was nearly gone. "Somehow, it seems . . ." Kyra bit her lip. Somehow, he was so easy to talk to that she had nearly blurted out her innermost feelings.

As he shifted to stare out the window, a blade of sunlight cut over his handsome face, accentuating the fine lines etched around his eyes by the rigors of war and its aftermath.

She looked away, reminding herself that she mustn't think of him as a kindred soul. Yes, that they had suffered loss of a loved one was an undeniable bond. But their situations were so achingly different.

"Somehow it seems unfair that you should be whole while a loved one is gone," he said after a few long moments. "Yes, I know. I feel just as you do. However, I have thought a great deal about that over the last five months, and have come to the conclusion that yes, life *is* terribly unfair, but I think both your sister and Jack would wish for us to live it to the fullest, as . . . as a celebration of their spirit."

Kyra pondered his words while the maid entered and set the tea tray on the table.

"It is not easy to push aside guilt," said Rafael once they were alone. "But please give some consideration to what I have said."

"I—I shall," she replied, for he was too kind for her to say otherwise. Though at heart, she couldn't imagine ever truly forgiving herself for what had happened.

"*Bueno*. And now we shall talk of more cheerful things." He helped himself to a strawberry tart and polished it off in three quick bites. "An idea occurred to me as I was walking here. I plan to return to London in a few days to purchase a few more supplies at the Covent Garden market."

She had wondered at the reason for his previous journey to London. There were, of course, any number of pleasures that would draw a gentleman to Town. *But shopping for foodstuffs?* His interests were so unusual—and intriguing. At times he appeared so solemn, so serious, then with mercurial quickness, a whimsical lightness could chase the shadows from his eyes.

His next words, however, jarred her from her musings.

"I thought perhaps you might care to accompany me. There is all manner of exotic produce sold there, including cacao pods from the Caribbean. So you could purchase some to paint here in your workroom."

The luscious shades of red and orange flashed in her mind's eye.

"And if you had your own pods, you would be free to cut them open and try your hand at depicting the interior, which has an interesting range of creamy colors."

The suggestion was oh-so tempting. But Kyra shook her head. "Thank you, but I don't intend to return to London." *Ever.*

"I understand your reluctance." Rafael rose and went to stand by the glass-paned doors. Unlike most bucks of the *ton*, he didn't feel the need to pontificate or push his point of view on his listeners. He was comfortable with silence and his own thoughts. It was one of the many things she found appealing about him.

Several more moments passed before he continued, "But be

assured that ladies like the marchioness and her daughters don't ever go to Covent Garden. It's filled with ordinary people—kitchen maids, hawkers, greengrocers, farmers, and seamen from all over the globe."

He paused, as if searching for the right words. "How to explain the atmosphere—it's noisy, it's bustling with a raucous energy. There's much good-natured haggling and cursing in a dozen different languages." His mouth curled up at the corners. "It will be fun. I promise."

"You make it sound—" Kyra looked around abruptly as the parlor door swung open.

"My dear. Oh, forgive me." The duke stopped short on the threshold. "I did not realize you had company."

"Papa, I don't believe you have yet met Lord Hendrie's nephew."

"Ah, the new Lord Leete." Pierpont approached and extended a hand. "Welcome, sir. Welcome."

Rafael accepted the greeting with good grace, though she could see that being called by Jack's title pricked like a thorn every time he heard it. "Thank you, Your Grace."

"His Lordship and I have met several times while out walking by the lake, Papa," explained Kyra. "And we also encountered each other at Kew Gardens. He has an interest in botany."

"Indeed?" Pierpont quickly masked his look of surprise. "A scholar as well as a soldier, I see."

"Merely a beginning student, though I confess that the subject does hold an allure for me. I am especially interested in *Theobroma cacao*, which is more commonly known as chocolate," Rafael explained, "I am trying to convince your daughter to come with me to the Covent Garden market in London, where it's possible to buy specimens."

The duke's brows shot up in surprise.

"It seemed that Lady Kyra found the plant interesting at Kew Gardens. And on the whole, the market is quite fascinating for an artist," added Rafael. "That is, Your Grace, if you have no objection."

The duke slanted a look at Kyra. "Why, I think that's quite a splendid idea, Leete."

"I am not sure your daughter agrees," said Rafael. "But I hope she will consider it."

He had painted such an appealing picture of the place. And it sounded as if she would be anonymous in the crowd.

No catty whispers, no hurtful snubs.

Kyra carefully collected the cups and plates and placed them back on the tray while her father and their visitor exchanged pleasantries about the local area. *Yes or no?* She knew the safe answer, the sensible answer.

Ah, but when did she ever choose caution over danger?

"I will," she finally announced. "Consider it, that is."

"Excellent." Rafael gave another glance at the engravings on the wall. "Did I mention there is a stand that sells potted orchids?"

"Orchids?" *Did the man possess magical powers?* How did he guess at her fascination with the delicate blooms?

"In a variety of colors."

Oh, definitely a warlock.

"Pink?" asked Kyra hesitantly.

"A deep, dusky pink, as I recall."

"When were you planning to make this trip, sir?"

"Ah, as to that, I have made no final plans. Is there a day that might suit you?"

"I am dispatching my under steward to Town to pick up a batch of books on agriculture from Hatchards on the day after tomorrow," said the duke. "The two of you could ride with him in the traveling coach. The new team of matched grays flies through the miles, so it will be an easy trip there and back."

Clasping his hands behind his back, Rafael raised one dark brow in question, waiting for her to answer.

"I . . ."

Her father looked to be holding his breath.

"I have to admit that I find the prospect of cacao and orchids too tempting to resist."

"Then it's settled!" Seeing her father's jaw unclench was worth the doubts that still roiled inside her. Perhaps it had been an error of judgment to agree. But there were already enough mistakes chalked on her slate that one more really wouldn't make any difference.

"It is getting late, so I had best be returning to Hendrie Hall." Rafael inclined a small bow to both of them. "Thank you for your hospitality to an uninvited guest."

"Nonsense. You need never stand on ceremony, Leete," replied the duke. "Our neighbors are always welcome here." He beckoned for Rafael to follow him. "Come, I shall show you out as I have a book that I would like to send along with you for your uncle."

Kyra rose to bid him farewell.

As Rafael passed, he said, "Wear old clothes and be prepared to enjoy yourself."

~

"WATCH YOUR STEP," counseled Rafael as they made their way along narrow cobbled passageway leading up from the Strand. "There are a great many substances underfoot that I don't care to identify."

"Ah." An ominous *squish* emanated from beneath Kyra's half boot. "I believe that was a rotten cabbage."

"I didn't realize your botanical expertise extended to vegetables." He grinned, happy to see she was taking the adventure in stride. "I would have guessed it was a turnip."

"No, there were definitely leaves involved."

Shadows flitted overhead. Only a dappling of sunlight penetrated the overhanging eaves, making the space seem even more pinched. Sounds were funneling down from the market, an ever-loudening cacophony of shouts and thumps amplified by the soot-dark brick of the buildings pressing in around them.

Rafael slanted a surreptitious look at Kyra, but saw only curiosity rather than trepidation shading her profile. A good sign, but she had yet to be swept up in the helter-pelter jostling of the crowds.

"It's best if we stay close together," he counseled, shifting the wicker basket from one hand to the other in order to take her arm. "The market is quite large, and with all the rows of stalls, it's easy to lose one's way."

A last turn took them through a low archway, and then, in a flash, they emerged from the gloom and into the bright sunlight.

"Oh." A sudden exhale escaped her lips as Kyra blinked, her eyes adjusting to the blaze of colors and whirlwind of activity.

"It's a bit chaotic," said Rafael, trying to gauge her reaction. "But cheerfully so." Or so he hoped, suddenly worried that he might have misjudged just how overwhelming the experience would seem to someone who had chosen to retreat into the shadows of solitude.

She didn't answer right away, which was further cause for concern. Inwardly cursing himself for a fool, he fumbled for something to say that might sooth her fears . . .

When all of a sudden, a smile tugged at the corners of her mouth. "There is so much to see—I hardly know which way to look."

"Let's begin here," answered Rafael quickly. Taking her arm, he guided her to a row of fruit stalls. "They have oranges from Valencia here. Their sun-kissed sweetness reminds me of home."

A woman clad in brightly mismatched calico hefted a sack of the plump fruits. "Aye. A handsome treat fer a handsome gent!" She winked at Kyra. "Ain't you a lucky gel."

Rafael promptly handed over some coins. "The luck is all mine, milady."

The fruit seller chortled. "Oh, sure enough, I be the Countess of Lemons and Limes." She raised several more sacks and winked. "Or would ye prefer some tasty English apples?"

"Just the oranges for now." He began peeling one of the fruits as he nudged Kyra to continue along the line of stalls. Their progress was greeted by good-natured jests and urgings to try more of the treats. Rafael purchased some almonds and sultanas, then led them down an aisle featuring pots and pans.

"Here, you must taste this." He handed Kyra a segment of peeled orange. "Close your eyes, and you can feel the warmth of the Spanish sun."

She hesitated, but only for an instant. "Mmmm. Why, that's quite delicious!"

"Have another morsel."

It disappeared even more quickly.

He peeled two more oranges and handed one of them to her. "I'm glad you like them. My grandmother had several trees in her garden and when I was a small child, it was always a special treat when she allowed me to choose one of the fruits."

"What lovely memories."

"Indeed." He hoped that she would soon let her own sunny memories of the past chase away the gloom of the recent events.

She looked thoughtful as she ate—slowly at first, then with increasing gusto. Her fingers were soon sticky and juice was dribbling down her chin. He reached out to flick a drop off her lower lip.

"Oh, Lud." A laugh burbled in her throat. "I must look like an absolute fright."

With her loosened curls dancing in the breeze, her cheeks flushed with mirth and her eyes sparkling with life, she had, in his estimation, never looked lovelier.

"You look like someone who appreciates oranges. As do I." He licked his syrupy fingers, drawing another laugh. "Have some

Marcona almonds. The saltiness is a nice counter to the sweetness of the oranges."

"Oh, I couldn't! I've indulged quite enough."

"Nonsense. It's impossible to indulge enough at markets. They are all about sampling everything."

"Well, if you insist."

A cheerful *crunch-crunch* punctuating their steps, they wended their way through the kitchenwares, the stacks of nubby linen and Belgian lace, and on to the flower stalls.

RAFAEL HAD NOT EXAGGERATED—THE display of orchids was even more impressive than he had described. Kyra stood entranced, the profusion of subtle hues and shapes leaving her a little breathless.

"Dare I hope the pinks are pleasing?" he asked.

"More than pleasing," she said. "They are astounding."

He stood for several long moments studying the blooms. "Let me try to guess which one you like best." Another drawn-out pause, before his fingers slid through the foliage, and drew one of the potted flowers closer. "I daresay it's this one."

"How did you guess?"

"I've seen your palette, remember? It's clear which shades of rose madder and alizarin crimson you favor."

"Most men would never notice such things," she mused.

"Ah, but I am not like most men."

How true. A clench of longing squeezed at her chest, but Kyra quickly shook it off. Such sentiments were now forbidden—she was no longer worthy of romantic dreams. Of romantic desires.

Ducking her head, she began fumbling in her reticle for her purse. "How much?"

Rafael stilled her hand. "Allow me to negotiate," he said softly. "Wait here."

He moved to the far end of the display, where the proprietor was busy trimming some yellowed leaves from a small ficus tree. A rapidfire series of gestures and grimaces ensued, then finally a gruff nod from the man. In answer, Rafael smiled and passed over some money.

"Sir, I can't allow you to pay for my purchase," said Kyra tightly when he returned. "How much do I owe you?"

A twinkle lit in his eyes. "Oh, never fear, I fully intended to ask for recompense for my bargaining skill. And it will cost you dear, Lady Kyra."

"How much?" she repeated, reaching back into her reticule.

"You have no need for your purse. I wish to be reimbursed with a watercolor sketch of the bloom."

"B-But that doesn't seem a fair exchange. Orchids are expensive—"

"Allow me to be the judge of that."

Kyra bit her lip, uncertain if it would be proper. God knows, she had transgressed enough of Society's rules for several lifetimes.

"I hope we might consider it an exchange of tokens of friendship," added Rafael.

Friendship. Surely even a fallen lady was allowed to have friends.

"Very well. But I still say I have gotten the best of the bargain." She reached for the flower.

"Mr. Wilkins says we may leave it here until we finish our shopping." He hefted his basket. "We need to visit the section where spices and exotic fruits and vegetables from the east and West Indies are on sale." Seeing she was loath to leave it, he added, "I've already made him swear a solemn oath not to sell it to anyone else."

A reluctant smile tugged at her lips. "It's a little unsettling how often you seem to read my thoughts. Does one of your grandmother's cacao recipes perchance confer the power of clair-voyance?"

"If so, I should bottle it and make my fortune selling it here in the market." Rafael flashed a boyish grin. "But alas, no. I have no special gifts."

Ha! His kindness and gentle humor were special beyond words. But as she shouldn't—nay, couldn't—say so, she merely averted her gaze. But strangely enough, in that blink of an eye, Kyra thought she saw a skirl of sadness flicker beneath his show of good cheer, as if he too, were masking some inner remorse or regrets.

Surely it must have been just a quirk of the light, for the handsome Spaniard was the very soul of honor and integrity.

Unlike me.

What possible pain could be tormenting his peace of mind?

He gave her no time to ponder the question. His smile firmly back in place, Rafael kept up a light-hearted commentary on all the sights, peppering his explanations of the various sections of the markets with droll observations that kept her chuckling despite her inner turmoil. By the time the last items on Rafael's list had been purchased, they had navigated nearly the entire twisting turns of the produce section.

"Sorry," he apologized. "I fear I have worn you out chasing down these vanilla pods from New Spain."

"Not at all," responded Kyra, though fatigue was starting to slow her steps. When she grew tired, her injured leg ached abominably, but she was determined not to show it. "I have learned more about New World botany from the last two fruit sellers than I have from a shelf of my Father's scholarly books."

"I don't know about you, but I am famished." Rafael spotted a nearby costermonger hawking his wares. "Ah, meat pasties! Just the sort of sustenance we need after trekking through the stalls."

Kyra was about to protest that she wasn't hungry when she realized that she was. Indeed, the scent wafting up from the man's barrow was making her mouth water. She started to follow Rafael when a sudden tangling of her skirts nearly caused her to trip.

Looking down, she saw a dark shape wiggle free of the muslin folds. With its matted fur, torn ear and oversized paws, there was nothing remotely cuddly about the scrawny puppy, but as their eyes met, topaz mixing with emerald in the wink of sunlight, she felt a lump form in her throat.

"Oh, sweetheart. You're hurt . . ." As her fingers grazed its mud-encrusted tail, a stone thumped against the puppy's ribs.

"Cripple!' An urchin, nearly as filthy as the dog, scampered around one of the stalls and hurled another stone. "Cripple!" Two other lads appeared as well, and added a peltering of rotten apples.

"Stop!" cried Kyra, shifting to shield the puppy as the leader of the pack raced in and aimed a kick at its rump.

The blow glanced off her shin, causing her to lose her footing and fall to the ground.

With a frightened yelp, the puppy bolted off and squeezed through a gap between two big wooden casks just as its tormenter lunged for its tail.

"Don't let it escape!" yelled the urchin to his friends. Slippery as eels, they darted through the gathering crowd and chased after their quarry.

CHAPTER 7

*R*afael spun around at the sound of Kyra's cry. He saw her tangle with the urchin and go down, but what with the jumble of crates and the press of onlookers crowding in, it took him a moment to reach her side.

"What happened?" he asked as he reached down to help her up from the muddy ground.

She brushed away his hand. "Never mind me—please, you must save the dog!" she gasped. "They mean to harm it!"

"Those little spawns of the devil are always making trouble," added the man at the neighboring stall. "They hared off that way." A wave of his pipe indicated one of the alleyways heading toward Seven Dials and the rookies of St. Giles.

"Please!" repeated Kyra

Gentlemanly scruples made him hesitate, but the note of emotion in her voice persuaded him. It was far more than anger, far more than outrage.

It was desperate need, as if saving some forlorn little animal was sort of penance for the past.

"Stay here," he ordered. Dropping the heavily-laden basket beside her, he turned and pelted off after the urchins.

Pushing his way free of the crowd that had gathered around them, Rafael swerved through the parade of shoppers, ignoring the aggrieved curses and the pain shooting through his own injured limb.

Dios Madre, if it would bring a smile to her face, he would run to the very depths of Hell and back.

The alleyways began to narrow and twist like the Devil's own tail. Clenching his teeth, he lengthened his stride. The uneven cobbles gave way to malodorous muck, making it even harder to keep his footing. His boots were slipping and sliding, yet still, through the grimy shadows he could see that he was managing to close the distance between him and the three urchins.

The leader of the pack ventured a glance over his shoulder and, seeing their pursuer closing in, he squeaked out an order to abandon the chase and darted down a side passageway, his companions following hot on his heels.

Rafael slowed, and then swore as a rotten apple sailed out from the gloom in a parting shot and knocked his hat into a mound of foul-smelling garbage. After taking another squishy step or two in its direction, he decided to leave it where it was.

Chest heaving, he sucked in a lungful of the fetid air and slowly looked around.

Now that the predators were dealt with, time to find the prey.

"Imps of Satan," exclaimed Kyra in a ragged gasp as she stumbled to a halt behind him. "Oh, I fear your hat is quite ruined."

"My hat is not my primary concern at the moment," replied Rafael. To his eye, she appeared too pale beneath the flush of exertion, and she looked to be favoring her bad leg, though she was taking great pains to hide it. "You should have stayed in the market." He knew it would only add to her agitation to mention her injury. "This area is not safe for a lady."

"Be damned with my safety," she uttered under her breath. "It's horrid that a defenseless little dog be frightened half to death by those boys." Tears pearled on her lashes. "And now the poor thing is hopelessly lost—"

"We'll find him." It was, he knew, a reckless promise to make but at that moment he was ready to take apart the surrounding rookeries brick by crumbling brick.

Kyra looked around uncertainly. "But I don't see how, sir."

"Nonetheless, we shall try." Taking her hand, he led the way a little farther into the stygian depth of the alleyway. All around, the shadows seemed to take on menacing shapes, and the creak of the overhanging eaves bounced evil echoes off the sooty walls.

The threat seemed so palpable that it seemed like a fist pressing against his chest. But he was not afraid of confronting physical danger.

He let out a little whistle and called to the dog in Spanish. "Hallooo, *Amigo!*"

Was it his imagination, or did a faint *woof* sound in answer?

Kyra, too, cocked an ear. "Did you hear something?"

Rafael called again.

The sound was a little louder, and seemed to be coming from just beyond the next turn.

"This way." Keeping firm hold of her hand, he edged forward, muscles tensed, his senses on full alert for any lurking menace. They rounded the bend, only to find the tumbled-down ruins of a wood and brick storage shed blocking half of the way.

A timid bark, follow by a whimper.

Kyra dropped to her knees, heedless of the ooze seeping through her skirts. "I think I see him," she said, peering between the splintered slats. "He looks to have fallen through a hole in the floor boards."

Woof, woof.

"I-I fear he may be trapped."

One look at her stricken expression and without a word, he stripped off his coat. "Kindly hold this." The gap in the rotten boards was just large enough for him to try squeezing through it.

"You mustn't, sir," she protested, casting a dubious look at the sagging timbers. "It's too dangerous."

Crouching down, Rafael surveyed the wreckage. On close inspection, there looked to be a way to crawl through the jumbled wood and brick without bringing the whole structure toppling down.

"I'll be careful." He had already rolled onto his back and was inching under the jutting beam. Was he mad to risk his life for a mangy mongrel? Saving a nameless stray wouldn't bring Jack back from the dead.

And yet, against all reason, the task had become a touchstone, a talisman of sorts to prove that hope could triumph over despair.

Holding his breath, he slowly slithered through a treacherous tangle of broken rafters. The dog's woofs had stopped, and the ensuing silence only amplified the ominous cast of the ink-dark shadows shrouding the depths of the wreckage.

Just a little farther, he calculated, making his way by touch rather than sight to the spot where the animal was trapped. *Slowly, slowly.* The mud was chill, the splinters sharp against his fingertips, but he dared not rush.

At last, his hand brushed up against a coarse curling of fur. He felt the dog stir and as a wet warmth licked against his skin, he chuffed a sigh of relief.

"*Si, si, amigo*, I am happy to meet you, too. But let us leave off formal introductions until I have you safely out of here." Rafael felt around and found where the dog's paw had become trapped within a crack in the floorboard. "Try to stay still."

The dog whined but ceased its struggling.

Splinter by splinter, he gingerly pried away at the half-rotten wood, slowly widened the opening just enough to release the prisoner. The dog scrabbled forward and nuzzled Rafael's cheek, and despite his bleeding palms and bruised shoulders, he couldn't repress a grin.

"I've got him, all is well," he called to Kyra. Which was, he admitted wryly, a bit of an exaggeration. To retreat without bringing the heavy timbers crashing down on their heads would be no easy feat.

"Oh, please be very careful," she whispered softly, as if afraid the merest breath would cause the wreckage to collapse.

"I—" One of the beams shivered at the touch of his boot, and emitted an ominous groan. "I assure you, I have no intention of sticking my spoon into the wall just yet."

Holding the dog tight to his chest, Rafael backtracked with painstaking precision through the maze of debris. His shirt suffered several rips, his trousers were caked in mud, and his cravat caught on a loose nail and was lost along the way. But somehow he emerged unscathed.

"You had better keep your distance until my *amigo* and I have had a bath," he said dryly as he levered to his feet. "Or maybe two. *Dios mio*, it will likely take a hogshead of soap to scrub the stench—"

Ignoring his warning, Kyra flung her arms around his shoulders. "Oh, sir, you are a true hero! You deserve a medal for valor!"

A muffled bark seemed to second the accolade.

Her smudged smile was reward enough. Rafael knew what an odd picture they must present, standing there spattered with grime, hugging a half-starved stray. Still, he couldn't help feeling absurdly proud of himself.

"Hardly." Mindful of ruining her clothing, Rafael tried to gently fend her away. "There is nothing heroic about crawling around in the muck."

Her eyes flared open at the sight of his scraped and bleeding hand. "Dear Lord, you're hurt!"

"Just a few scratches. It's nothing."

A strange heat suddenly thrummed against his skin as Kyra pressed her palm to his cheek. It was as if some powerful magnetic force was holding them flesh to flesh.

He couldn't move. He couldn't speak.

~

"Y-Your face is cut, too." Kyra had only meant to brush a bit of dirt from the nick on his cheekbone. But an elemental current seemed to take hold of her, and before she could think, before she could react, it drew her closer, closer . . .

Close enough to see the subtle play of hues swirling in the depths of his sapphire blue eyes. Close enough to be mesmerized by the sweetly sinuous shape of his mouth.

Close enough to find her lips hovering just a hairsbreadth from his. "I've never seen anything more heroic in my life than what you just did. It was quite wonderful."

You are quite wonderful.

Kyra wasn't sure whether it was Rafael or she who moved—or whether some invisible magic brought them together in a gossamer kiss. For one exquisite instant, she simply savored the sculpted contours of his mouth, strong yet velvet-soft, and the sense of gentle warmth that suffused her senses.

Then, thank heavens, reason reasserted itself in the form of the squirming dog.

Shame made the wondrous warmth turn in a flash to a wicked burn. Ducking her head to hide her flaming face, Kyra fumbled with freeing the rescued stray from the tangled folds of fabric.

Through the scrim of her lashes, she saw that he, too, was looking embarrassed. And with good reason. Though he was too gentlemanly to say so, he was probably horrified at having a wanton jade wrap herself around him. At that moment, she would have given all the tea in China to have the ground beneath her open up and drop her straight to Canton.

"Halloo, sweetheart," she crooned, stroking the dog's floppy ears to keep from meeting his gaze.

"He needs a proper name," said Rafael.

To Kyra's surprise, he didn't back away from her, now that he was no longer ensnared.

"My guess," he went on, "is that this ragged little imp will grow into those ungainly paws. A Spanish *hombre* would be greatly shamed by being called 'Sweetheart.' I daresay an English one would feel much the same."

"You are sure it's a male?"

"*Si.*" A twinkle of amusement lit in his eyes. "Very sure."

Kyra did not ask him to elaborate. She thought for a moment. "Then I shall name him Hero. Surely no *hombre* could object to that."

"Hero." Rafael reached out and ruffled his fingers through the dog's matted fur. "Perhaps he will grow into his name as well as his paws."

"At least he will have a chance to prove himself." She hadn't really considered the ramifications of running after the half-starved dog. As was her wont, she had acted on impulse. But as Hero began to suckle and chew on her finger, the decision was oh-so clear.

"But first I must get him something to eat. He's starving." After running a hand over his protruding little ribs, Kyra added, "And a blanket for the carriage ride home."

She rather expected him to make all sorts of reasonable objections to adopting a scruffy stray.

But instead, Rafael merely nodded as he plucked his coat from where she had hung it on a protruding nail and tugged it on. It was cleaner than his torn shirt, Kyra noted thankfully, and would provide him with some protection from the damp chill that was settled over the alleyway now that the sun had passed its zenith.

"Here, let me carry him," he offered.

"But your coat, sir." Her nose crinkled as Hero rubbed his whiskered snout against her cheek. "We've already caused the ruin of your other clothing, not to speak of your boots." His valet would like swoon if asked to clean them. "And as you've discovered, he has some rather foul things encrusted in his fur."

"To the Devil with my coat," answered Rafael cheerfully. "I was never fond of this particular shade of grey. It will be vastly improved by mixing in a bit of brown." He lifted Hero from her arms, and was rewarded with a series of slobbering kisses to his chin. "Yes, yes, you smelly little imp, I rather like you, too." Unfazed by the needle-like teeth now attacking his lapels, he went on, "I think with some proper nourishment, he will make you a very fine country hound."

Kyra felt a surge of elation well up in her chest. "Oh, you truly think it is alright if we take him with us?"

"I don't see why not. He's clearly been abandoned."

"It is exceedingly kind of you to allow strays and outcasts to attach themselves to your . . ." She was suddenly aware of his steadying hold on her arm. ". . .Your coat."

"My coat is already greatly improved." A grin as he indicated the shredded fabric and missing button on his collar. "Perhaps, like your famous Beau Brummel, I shall start a new style in gentlemen's fashion." Rafael gave a mock wince as Hero nipped at his ear. "Shall we call it the Hungry Hound?"

Kyra laughed. "I know there are Tulips of the *ton* who spend hours in front of the mirror perfecting the knot of their cravats, but I am not sure they would be quite as tolerant as you are, not even for the sake of appearing an arbiter of style."

"You underestimate the vanity of most men," he said.

No, thought Kyra. *I don't.* Which was why Rafael de Villafranca Greeley was so . . .

How to describe him? No single word seemed adequate to capture the complexity of his character. Whimsical, yet serious. Strong, yet sensitive . . . reserved, yet kind, handsome as sin, yet—

She made her stop.

"Have a care, Lady Kyra." His grip kept her upright as she

stumbled over a broken crate. "Another turn and we will be out of the alleyways."

They walked on in companionable silence and were soon back to the bustle of the Covent Garden market. The man selling meat pies from his barrow had promised Kyra to keep their shopping basket, and as they approached to collect it, the vendors at the nearby stalls seemed highly bemused by their disheveled appearance.

"All that trouble for a flea-bitten cur?" The turnip seller scratched his bulbous nose. "Seems daft te me."

"Aye," agreed the fellow selling smoked hams. "Look at them garments—they ain't fit for aught but the rag picker anymore."

"That may be true," Kyra said as she slanted yet another look at Hero's lolling tongue and blissful expression as he bestowed another lick to Rafael's chin. "But I consider their demise well worth it."

"Perhaps the wee doggie is a Royal favorite, and they are going to receive a king's ransom as a reward," chimed in the dairy merchant. "Ha, ha, ha."

A chorus of laughter followed.

"Looks to me like the ragged little rascal is more likely a Royal pain in the arse," muttered the turnip seller, which sparked even more hilarity.

Rafael grinned at the teasing. "Oh, come, you have to admit the scamp is rather endearing." He held up Hero, who wagged his scruffy tail. "Or will be once he puts a little meat on his bones."

"Scrawny runt, ain't he?" The ham vendor looked at Kyra and cleared his throat. "Here, I've a few scraps for him."

"I suppose I can spare a bit of milk," piped up the dairy merchant.

"Here, ye can add some of these stale crusts to the milk," offered a woman selling bread. "But mind, missy, not te feed him too much at once, else he'll shoot the cat."

"Shoot the cat?" She glanced at Rafael, who seemed equally puzzled.

"Cast up his accounts," explained the ham vendor as he held out a piece of oiled paper piled with a generous helping of meaty scraps.

"Sick to his stomach," added the costermonger

"Ah." Rafael nodded.

"Feed him slowly," counseled the woman.

Hero seemed to sense he was the center of attention and played shamelessly to his audience, eating with surprisingly genteel manners and whuffling contented little noises as he shifted his skinny body on his oversized paws.

The crowd was quickly won over, and a pelter of advice and suggestions followed on how much he should be fed at the present moment, and what should be done to keep him comfortable during the carriage ride to the country. A blanket appeared, along with a battered bowl for water, and by the time she and Rafael were ready to take their leave with their new companion, they had made fast friends with the vendors.

"Come back soon, missy and bring yer Hero with ye," said the bread woman. She pressed an extra package of crusts into Kyra's hands, along with several fragrant sultana muffins wrapped in a square of paper for her and Rafael to enjoy during the trip home. "And yer handsome gent," she added in a lower voice.

"We will," she promised, trying not to blush. "And thank you all for your kindness." With them, she hadn't been treated as a reviled outcast, a subject of sidelong stares and nasty whispers.

"Indeed," said Rafael. He had, she noticed, discreetly passed out a generous number of coins to all those who had offered to share their wares. "Though the next time you lay eyes our little imp, he will likely be as big as an ox."

More laughter and cheery waves as they took their leave, a contented Hero already fast asleep in Rafael's arms.

"Wait, we have one more stop to make," he said as she started toward the passageway leading back down to the Strand.

"Surely we've acquired enough items for one trip," said Kyra, unable to hold back a small frown. "Besides, I doubt you could fit one more thing in that basket." She had offered to carry it, noting that his leg seemed to be troubling him, but he had refused.

"Your orchid."

She had completely forgotten about the bloom.

"We can't leave that behind."

That he had remembered, despite all the tumult of the chase, brought a lump to her throat. "We can, and we will," said Kyra softly, "unless you will allow me to carry it. I won't have another burden weighing down your . . ."

She nearly said 'step,' but caught herself.

"Arms," she finished lamely.

"My arms are stronger than they look, Lady Kyra."

"Nonetheless, I insist."

"*Bueno*," said Rafael after a slight hesitation. "I learned from my Grandmother not to argue with a lady when she gets that glint in her eye."

In short order, the orchid was collected and they made their way back to where the duke's carriage was waiting. The coachman's face betrayed a spasm of surprise at their raggle-taggle appearance, but he quickly cleared it away with a brusque cough —or was it a laugh—and jumped down from his perch to help them with all their various items.

"The basket may go in the boot, John," said Kyra. "But have a care that you pad it well so it doesn't get too jostled during the journey."

"Aye, milady." His nose gave an involuntary twitch. "As for that . . . er, animal, would you care to have it ride out in the open air with me?"

"No, no, we shall tend to the dog ourselves," replied Rafael.

"Dog, is it?" the coachman asked as he took charge of the

basket. "Very good, sir. Just, er, give a rap on the trap if you need me to stop anywhere along the way." His brows rose a fraction higher as he eyed the exotic orchid. "As for the, er, flower, milady."

"Oh, we shall tend to that as well," answered Kyra.

The coachman looked rather relieved.

"And now," she added, seeing Hero was stirring, "perhaps it would be best if we set off without further delay."

"Er, just one last thing, milady . . ." The coachman fetched a clean blanket from the boot and carefully spread it over the pristine tufted upholstery of the interior seat.

Once settled on the protective covering, Kyra leaned back against the squabs and let out a long exhale. "What a day."

"Indeed, yet I trust that you mean it in a good way," responded Rafael as he stretched out his long legs.

"Selfishly yes. But . . ." Despite the flitting shadows, she thought she caught a grimace of pain pull at his mouth. "But your leg must be hurting abominably, what with all the trouble I've put you through!"

He flexed his knee and looked a bit bemused. "Oddly enough, it doesn't. It's a trifle stiff, but the pain seems to have disappeared." His gaze angled down to her rumpled skirts. "And what of you, Lady Kyra? You, too, pushed yourself very hard, and must be hurting."

Good heavens, she hadn't given her bad leg a thought.

In truth, for the first time since the accident, she felt something akin to her old self. The bustling thrum of the market, the cheerful banter with the vendors, the spark of passion roused by the injured dog's plight—it had all drawn her out of her lethargy and made her feel alive again.

Passion. The recollection of her impulsive kiss made her shift uncomfortably on the seat.

"I am suffering no ill effects from my physical exertions," said Kyra carefully. "Indeed, all the expensive experts Papa has consulted would likely say it was beneficial for my health."

"*Bueno,*" he began.

"But," she interrupted, "I fear all the running may have momentarily jumbled my wits." A pause as she pondered just how to apologize for throwing herself at him. "I hope you will forgive my unseemly display of emotion in the alleyway. I was so happy about Hero."

It seemed to take several long, drawn-out moments for him to piece together her meaning. His reply, when it finally came, was far less oblique.

"Are you perchance apologizing for kissing me?"

"Well, yes, that was the general idea," she admitted. Another pause. "Though it was more of an embrace than a kiss."

"An embrace?" His brows waggled up a notch. "No, no—I have experienced both, and it was definitely a kiss."

"You were distracted. By the dog."

Hero started to squirm in his lap. "True. But be assured that even had I been distracted by a Bengal tiger or a dancing bear, I would not have mistaken a kiss for an embrace."

That she found bantering with him so enjoyable made her feel even more guilty. "Then the mistake is all mine," she said tightly. "I have somehow given you the wrong impression. So again, I am offering you my apology."

"None is necessary. I was simply teasing, but I see that I've upset you. Please—"

"I am not upset," she said quickly. "I am merely fatigued."

"Understandably so." Rafael unwrapped the muffins and held one out as a peace offering of sorts. "We both have been run a little ragged by our four-footed *amigo*. Perhaps a bit of sustenance would help restore our strength."

Hero sniffed the air and let out a little whine.

"Not you, imp," he scolded. "You've already eaten enough for a regiment of the King's Hussars." To Kyra he added, "Any more, and I fear an unfortunate accident might befoul your Father's pristine carriage."

His words signaled a tactful end to the awkward interlude. Relieved, she quickly responded, "Quite right—Hero can't possibly be famished, but I am. And those muffins smell divine."

The talk turned to cooking and Rafael's mellifluous voice was calming, the mellow tones softened even more by the dark wood paneling and flickering carriage lamp. As he chatted on at great length about the recipes he had recently translated and which ones he intended to try with his purchases from the market, Kyra nibbled at her sultana-studded pastry, feeling the knot in her stomach slowly loosen.

"You must be sure to tell me how your creations turn out," she said, as he paused to take a bite of his muffin.

"Oh, but I am hoping you will agree to come sample them with me," he replied. "I have promised to accompany Uncle Aubrey to Newmarket on the morrow, to help him purchase a pair of hunters for the stables. We shall be gone for five or six days, but when I return, I shall set to work."

"That would be lovely. Your grandmother's chocolate recipes are too tempting a treat to resist."

"Excellent!" He tickled a sleepy Hero under his whiskered chin. "Sweets are not good for dogs, but I shall have some nice meaty bones for you."

A short while later, the carriage crested a hill and turned up the sloping drive of Hendrie Hall. Rafael settled the dog in Kyra's lap, then reached for the door latch as the wheels slowed to halt by the main portico.

"Thank you for a memorable experience," she said as he prepared to descend the iron rungs.

He looked back and grinned, the lingering streak of mud on his left cheek giving his face a lopsided cant. "Our Grand Tour of the market took a few unexpected twists and turns. But some-times the unexpected adds a certain spice to life."

Or a certain pinch of painful regret. She had never expected to regain an appetite for life. She had never expected to feel the rekindling of love in the ashes of her heart.

If only . . .

Looking down at the dozing dog, Kyra nodded. "So it does," she said, trying hard to match the lightness of his tone. He must never guess at her true feelings. His kindness was hard enough to bear. His pity would be intolerable.

"Safe travels, sir," she went on. "And when you return, I look forward to seeing what magic you create in the kitchen with your spices and sugar—and your cacao, of course."

No matter that bitter taste of her past folly would always rise up to spoil the sweetness.

CHAPTER 8

"*Dios Mio*. Perhaps he's half horse." Rafael chuckled as Hero raced over across the terrace, paws slipping and sliding on the flagstones, and jumped up with an enthusiastic greeting that left a trail of mud on his biscuit-colored breeches. "Surely a normal canine couldn't grow that much in six days!"

"Down, boy," chided Kyra, her voice a bit breathless from hurrying to catch hold of the dog's collar. "I'm so sorry. He's really been quite good about learning his manners, however . . ." She brushed a lock of hair from her flushed cheek. "However, he's very happy to see you."

Rafael couldn't help but wonder whether Hero's owner had similar sentiments, but the poke of her chip straw bonnet hid her eyes. "Well, I am very happy to see him, too," he answered. "He looks and feels like he's put on a stone since last week."

A smile flickered on her lips. "That's because he eats like a horse, even if he's all dog."

"At least he no longer resembles a sewer rat." The dog's curling grey fur was surprisingly silky against his palm.

"Papa thinks he's some sort of mixed breed hunting hound—perhaps part Scottish deerhound and part long-haired pointer."

Rafael carefully extricated his hand from Hero's overexuberant embrace. "I can believe it. He has *very* strong jaws."

"Oh, fie, Hero! Behave yourself!" scolded Kyra. "That's a *very* shabby way to treat your rescuer. His Lordship's fingers are *not* breakfast treats."

Sitting back on his haunches, the hound flattened his ears and looked as contrite as a blissfully happy animal could manage.

"I think we may excuse his table manners for the moment," said he dryly. "Given his previous hardscrabble existence, we cannot blame him for kicking up his heels a bit."

"He does seem to have taken to country life with great enthusiasm. Papa's kennel master mixed a poultice for his hind leg and the cut is almost healed. You ought to see him frolic over the grounds." The sparkle in her eyes grew as animated as the hound's thumping tail. "Chasing rabbits, splashing after swans in the river." A low laugh. "Digging up several of the head gardener's freshly planted rose bushes."

Rafael wagged a stern finger. "We shall have to train you to obey some basic commands, *amigo*. A proper gentleman must master polite behavior if he wishes to be a welcome guest. Now pay attention."

Hero sat up and cocked his head.

"Come."

The dog obediently trotted over . . .

"You see, this will be easy. He is a very smart—"

And promptly piddled on his boot.

Kyra dissolved in a fit of giggles.

Giving a mock grimace of horror to stifle his own mirth, Rafael uttered a few choice words in Spanish at the dog, and was rewarded with a canine grin before Hero bounded away to nose around in the nearby flowerbeds. "I see we shall have to instigate a more disciplined training regimen for the beast."

"Yes," she agreed. "But for the moment, let us allow him the freedom to frolic a little. He deserves it."

He watched the gold-flecked sparkles of sunlight play along the curl of her lashes. "Yes, frolicking is important."

She didn't respond right away. For an instant it seemed as if a shadow passed over her face, but then she turned and it was gone.

"I didn't stop by this morning merely to ruin yet another item of your wardrobe." Her mouth twitched as she shot a quick glance at his befouled boot. "I wanted to give you this."

Rafael accepted the small paper-wrapped package.

"As payment," she added softly. "My father has always taught me that an honorable person does not delay in discharging a debt."

"You are not in my debt," he said softly. If anything, he owed her more than he could express for helping him to climb out from the darkest depths of despair.

Kyra and chocolate. They had reminded him that life, with all its bitter pain and heartache, was still sublimely sweet.

"We agreed to exchange tokens of friendship," he added.

"Call it what you will." Her taut whisper was nearly swallowed in the breeze. "We made a bargain, and I wish to fulfill my obligation."

Friendship implied a certain degree of intimacy, and clearly she was intent on keeping a distance from men, despite the fleeting moments that drew them together. Sensing her skittishness, Rafael said nothing further—yet he couldn't help but utter a silent oath at the cad who had shattered her trust.

Shattered her innocence.

Damn. Damn. Damn.

The ribbon slipped free and the paper fell away, revealing a watercolor painting encased in a simple wood frame.

In contrast to the uncertainty etched on every delicate curve and contour of her face, the brushstrokes were rendered with a deft confidence that captures the orchid and all its nuanced hues to perfection. Or perhaps it was even better than perfection, he mused. The exquisite details, the luminous colors, the subtle shadings—in her hands, pigment and paper were magically transformed into a stunning work of art.

Kyra finally ventured to break the silence between them. "If you don't like it, I can do another one."

"It's marvelous," replied Rafael.

The rigid set of her shoulders relaxed ever so slightly.

"Truly marvelous. You have a very special talent."

Another flicker of a shadow.

Praise, he noted, seemed to make her uncomfortable. Shrugging it off, she quickly changed the subject. "And what of you? Have you delved into your market basket and begun any new cacao creations yet?"

"I had just begun laying out all the ingredients in the kitchens and was going to send word to the manor asking if you cared to join me for a cooking session this morning."

"That would be lovely. Last night I started sketching the cacao pods I purchased at the market, and I confess that the luscious colors and fragrance made me think about your Grandmother's recipes." The corners of her mouth twitched upward. "Which led me to brew up a late night treat of hot chocolate."

"I've copied out some far more intriguing recipes than frothed milk and powdered cacao. What say you we give them a try?"

At Kyra's nod, Rafael turned and whistled for Hero. "I've a nice meaty bone, which should keep him out of trouble."

As for his own wayward thoughts . . .

He couldn't stop recalling her halting apology for kissing him. *Damnation!* He didn't want apologies. He wanted her to enjoy their budding friendship as much as he did.

No guilt, no shadows of recrimination. Over the last several weeks, he had come to realize that remaining imprisoned by the past only allowed Darkness yet another victory over Hope and Joy.

Jack would not have wished that.

Nor, he guessed, would Kyra's sister.

Kyra's laugh drew him from his inner reveries. "Trouble!" she repeated as the dog bounded across the terrace, beheading a swath of potted geraniums with his wagging tail. "I fear our four-footed friend has a knack for getting into trouble."

"And I have a knack for getting him out of trouble, so we are well matched." Rafael offered his arm. "Shall we go in?"

THE COLORS and scents were a feast for the senses. Kyra paused for a moment, drinking it all in, before following Rafael to the large worktable set in the center of the kitchen. After settling Hero in a corner by the stove, happily gnawing on the promised bone, he took up a fine-tooth grater and began shaving nutmeg into a bowl.

"What can I do to help?" she asked.

Her question seemed to take him by surprise. "You can chop these." He passed over a small dish of shelled walnuts, along with a cleaver. "Have a care—the blade is very sharp."

She liked that he didn't assume she was a helpless widget, who had never lifted a finger to do some ordinary task. It made her feel . . .

No, she wasn't going to spoil the pleasant interlude by brooding.

Taking up the cleaver, she set to work. "How small do you wish the pieces?"

"Those are perfect." Rafael looked up through his dark lashes. "You did not tell me you were an experienced cook."

"I'm not. But I often make infusions and tisanes from the

herbs and healing plants I collect in the forests. So I've learned to wield a knife and a mortar and pestle."

"A lady of many talents," he said. "Here, since you so adept with kitchen implements, kindly cut up this orange and squeeze out three measures of juice into the glass by your side.

They worked together at the chopping block in companionable silence for a short interlude, then Rafael took down a copper sauce pan from the overhanging rack and moved to the stove. As she minced a piece of peeled ginger, she watched him mix a chunk of creamy butter with a cupful of pungent sugar from Barbados and put it on the hob to heat. He added the tiny seeds from a pod of vanilla and began stirring. In several moments the room was filled with a mouth-watering fragrance.

"What are you making?'

"A caramel confection. First, I melt the sugar and butter and cook it over a low heat until it turns a rich golden brown. Then I'll add the chopped walnuts and let it cool to a toffee-like consistency. Lastly, I—that is, we, assuming you would like to help—will form small balls of the mixture and dip them in melted chocolate."

"That sounds absolutely heavenly."

"There is a reason the Aztecs called chocolate the food of the Gods." He dipped his finger in the simmering sugar, and turning to the table extended his hand. "Here, would you like to try a taste now?"

Perhaps it was the combination of moist heat, heady scents and softly flickering sunlight spilling through the leaded windows that created the irresistible enchantment. Whatever the unseen force, Kyra found herself powerless to resist. She leaned in and flicked out her tongue.

"Mmmm." Closing her eyes, she sighed as she savored the seductive sweetness. A buttery warmth seemed to melt through her limbs, and all at once she felt light as a feather, floating on a sun-kissed tropical breeze.

Oh, wouldn't it be heavenly to always feel so free! Unweighted by careless mistakes . . .

A light touch of his fingertip to her lower lip brought her out of her reverie. "You must finish the rest. It's too delicious to waste a drop."

Her lids flew open and at the sight of his oh-so sensuous mouth close to hers, Kyra recoiled.

Rafael leaned back, his smile pinching to a look of dismay. A spark of emotion flashed for an instant, turning his smoky blue gaze to a hard-edged sapphirine glitter. *Anger? Or hurt?* The smoldering look that lingered was impossible for her to decipher.

He muttered something in Spanish, then switched to English. "Am I so very repulsive or threatening?" he demanded. "Whenever I get close, you pull away as if . . . as if I have sprouted horns and cloven hooves."

She drew in a ragged breath, searching her benumbed brain for words to explain.

"Not all men are devils," he added softly.

"It's not *you*," stammered Kyra. "It's *me*."

"You?"

"Yes, me!" She backed up another step. "You are good and honorable, and far too kind to me. I . . . I don't deserve it."

Rafael's expression softened. "Why don't you let me be the judge of that, *querida*?"

"Because you don't know the truth." A harsh exhale. "Oh, I don't doubt that you've heard the rumors—*all* the rumors."

"*Si*, I have heard them. People have vicious tongues.

"Trust me, they are too kind by half."

"Lady Kyra—"

"Truly they are. I—"

A sudden commotion in the entrance hall cut her off. A door slammed followed by a shout.

"Uncle Aubrey!" Rafael spun around and nearly tripped over Hero, who had been roused by their heated exchange. "He's been looking a little unwell of late." Dodging the gamboling dog, he raced past the pantries and down the corridor.

Kyra threw down her paring knife and ran after him, followed by Hero tagging along at her heels.

The wall sconces flickered wildly, casting dark-fingered shadows across the wainscoting. The noises grew louder—a jumble of voices as housekeeper and butler tried to talk at once.

Fearful that the earl had indeed been stricken ill, Kyra quickened her pace. Word was that he had been suffering from a weak constitution, but she feared the true cause of his ailment was not entirely physical.

Could one pass away from a broken heart?

Turning the corner, she nearly collided with Rafael, who had stopped short in archway. His whole body had gone rigid, as if carved out of steel.

Or ice. He looked frozen in place.

A clench seized her chest, making it hard to breath, and the voices of the servants seemed to fade to a faraway mumble. Still, she made herself duck around him to see what had happened.

Her gaze swept over the checkered tiles, but instead of finding a body, she saw only a pair of the very worn and very dusty boots.

The housekeeper burst into tears.

Kyra raised her eyes. *Ragged buckskins, none too clean, a tattered coat, whose broad-shouldered bulk only accentuated the painfully thin limbs of the scarecrow wearing it, unkempt hair in dire need of a trim, a topaz twinkle beneath dark wing-shaped brows . . .*

Of all the gentlemen she had met, only one had eyes that exact hue of Baltic amber. Jack.

"Dear God in Heaven," she whispered.

"Nay, just a mere mortal, though I daresay I'm only a shade of my former self," replied a familiar voice. "Even so, I was expecting a rather more welcoming homecoming."

CHAPTER 9

"*Buen día*, cousin." The gaunt face angled toward Rafael, sparks of sunlight gilding the dark stubbled whiskers on the sunken cheeks. "Aren't you going to welcome me back from the dead?"

It *was* Jack. For a long, long moment, he hadn't dared believe it was aught but a fiendish hallucination, brought on by some inexplicable chemistry in the cooking cauldron. But on seeing the faint smile wreath the other man's face, the doubts dissolved.

One—two—three quick strides closed the gap between them and then his arms wrapped around Jack's bony shoulders in a fierce hug. "*Dios mío*! I thought . . . I searched the battlefield, but I was told . . ." Rafael's voice caught in his throat as he tightened his hold on his cousin, unashamed of the tears welling up in his eyes.

"Aye, I was told much later that the French searchers had searched the hill first, and after collecting their wounded, buried the dead in a mass grave. I was lucky—a French officer who was still alive had fallen atop me, and as they heard his groans and came to carry him away, they saw my legs twitch and took pity on me."

"Thank God for your having a guardian angel," rasped Kyra, who had taken a few tentative steps closer.

Jack grinned. "Rafael will no doubt insist it was his grandmother, Dona Maria, who was looking out for me. And it may well be. As a boy, I was always a little in awe of her magical powers."

"Whatever force of the cosmos, I shall offer up my fervent thanks." A pause. "And a cup of frothed Spanish chocolate as a sacrificial libation."

"I would rather you gave the chocolate to me," quipped Jack. "Given all your stories of cacao's healthful nourishing powers, I could use a cup or two."

"You'll have potfuls of hot chocolate, and I shall also stuff you with cacao confections made with butter and nutmeats." Aware of his cousin's jutting ribs and withered muscles, he loosened his embrace and gruffly added, "You need to put some meat on your bones."

"Confections?" Jack raised a ragged brow. "Does that mean your grandmother's journals did contain recipes—"

"Never mind that now." As the initial shock subsided, Rafael suddenly had a myriad questions bubbling up in his brain. "Why the devil didn't you write to let us know you were coming? Uncle Aubrey . . ."

Thank God the earl had not witnessed the door being opened to the ghostly apparition. His heart might not have survived the shock.

"I take it my letter didn't arrive." His cousin slanted a look at the still-weeping housekeeper, though her tears were now watering a joyful smile. "My apologies for giving you all such a fright. Had I known you had received no advance warning of my arrival, I would not have appeared like some specter from the Underworld." A shrug, which set the oversized coat to fluttering like the wings of a bat against his dusty boots. "My father . . ."

"Your Father is working in his study. I had better be the one to inform him of the joyous news," said Rafael quickly. "Seeing your phiz—especially in its current state—might put *him* in the grave instead of you."

"Come, let us await him in the drawing room," rasped Kyra as she placed a tentative hand on Jack's arm. "You ought not be on your feet." To the butler she added, "Please bring tea and some sustenance."

"Tea," Jack said. "I've missed that excellent English brew." A wry smile. "Along with a number of other things."

As his cousin allowed himself to be led away, Rafael turned and hurried down the corridor, trying to compose the appropriate words to tell a father that his dead son had come back to life.

Miracles do happen. The brutal realities of war had shattered many idealistic illusions he had had about life. But a moment like this one reaffirmed that a bright, pure light could penetrate even the blackest shroud of darkness.

A smile playing on his lips, Rafael knocked softly on the study door, then slowly eased it open.

"Forgive me for interrupting, Uncle Aubrey, but I have some news to share you with."

"Hmm?" Hendrie looked up from his book and the untidy pile of scribbled notes with a vague squint. "Oh, no apologies are necessary. An excuse to abandon this passage of Pindar is most welcome. It's deucedly difficult to translate ancient Greek humor into iambic pentameter." He pinched at the bridge of his nose, then removed his spectacles and polished the lenses on his sleeve before putting them back on. "So, have you discovered some hint of a new species of cacao in Dona Maria's journals?"

"Exciting as that moment would be," Rafael said, "this one is even better."

"Ah, well, then it must be momentous, indeed." Laying down his pen, Hendrie waited expectantly. Though he had forced a smile, Rafael couldn't help but note that his uncle's blue eyes seemed to be leaching color with every passing day. In the muted shadows, they appeared naught but a lifeless grey.

'Indeed it is." Rafael drew a chair close to the desk and sat down. "Though at first it may come as something of a shock . . ." An understatement if ever there was one. "So please prepare yourself."

"My dear boy, very little can shock me at this point in life." Though it was said with a humorous tone, a profound sadness shaded his uncle's voice."

"Suppose I were to tell you that the assumption of Jack's death was a mistake."

Hendrie went pale as the fragment of ancient Greek marble that graced his desk. Drawing in a ragged breath, he let it out in a whispered rush of words.

An oath? An exultation? They were too jumbled for Rafael to make out.

Lips trembling, the older man took a moment to compose himself before adding, "W-W-What are you saying?"

"That I've just learned our regiment's commanders were wrong."

Hendrie fumbled with his pen, then his spectacles, as if some talisman of his everyday life could help affirm that what he had just heard. "How can you be sure?" he croaked. "They might be wrong again."

"There's no mistake." Rafael reached out and twined his fingers around his uncle's frail wrist. He could feel the rapid-fire thud of the other man's heart pulsing beneath the warm flesh. "You see, Jack is here, having a cup of tea in the drawing room as we speak."

"Here? In the flesh?"

"More bones than flesh." All at once, a laugh welled up in Rafael's throat. "He looks like a wraith from Hell, and smells even worse. But yes, Uncle Aubrey, he is here."

Hendrie half rose and then fell back heavily to his chair.

And then they both burst into tears.

~

"Sit," commanded Kyra, leading Jack to one of the tufted overstuffed armchairs. "But first . . ." She grasped the coarse wool of his overcoat and gently eased it off his shoulders."

"Oh, aye, it *is* a rather foul garment, and Mrs. Ganton would birch my bottom if I were to soil her precious brocade." A sigh slipped from his lips as he slouched into the soft down cushions. "Ahhh. This is far more comfortable than the sack of turnips I sat on during the ride from Plymouth to Exeter."

She pushed over a hassock and lifted his legs one by one to rest on it.

"Had I known I would be waited on hand and foot, I might have stepped into a saber slash sooner," he quipped as she spread a soft merino throw over his lap.

"Do not get too accustomed to being treated like royalty," she replied tartly. "Whatever other bodily harm you have suffered, it's apparent that your annoying sarcasm escaped uninjured. So my sympathy will be short-lived."

"Alas, you wound me grievously." Exaggerating a soulful sigh, Jack placed a hand on his chest. "My heart aches at your unkind words."

"What fustian." Kyra plumped a pillow and placed it behind his head. "You don't have a heart, a fact that countless young ladies in London will happily attest to."

He laughed, and for an instant the harsh lines etched around his mouth softened, the dark hollows in his cheeks lightened, giving her a fleeting glimpse of the carefree young man who had marched so confidently off to war.

Looking away, she blinked back tears.

"You know me too well. I cannot pull the wool over your eyes, I see—you will always call me to account for my sins."

Kyra flinched at the word "sins."

Whether or not Jack noticed, he shifted and brushed a lock of lank hair back from his brow. "Since we are speaking with the frankness of old and dear friends, allow me to say that . . ."

She felt her skin hot and prickly under the intensity of his gaze.

"Hell's Bells, you look bloody awful," he finished. "What the devil happened?"

"An accident," replied Kyra. "A reckless horse race gone awry. Lexy is dead—and all because of me."

"I'm so very sorry."

She didn't dare look at him for fear her voice would crack into a thousand shards. "As am I."

"You were injured as well?" His eyes were still as sharp as ever. It was more a statement than a question

"A broken leg—and a shattered reputation." A wry grimace. "The leg is nearly mended. The reputation is most definitely not."

"Tell me what happened," he asked softly.

"You'll hear the sordid story soon enough. But in a nutshell, I'm considered fast, in every sense of the word. After my unbridled rashness in accepting a racing wager with Lord Pemberton, rumors began to circulate that I was a . . . fallen woman."

"I don't believe it—"

"Of course you do," she interrupted roughly. "You know I've always been reckless to a fault."

"High-spirited and independent," he corrected.

Kyra bit her lip. "Which has led to my ruin. My fiancé cried off as a result, so I am an outcast, shunned by Society."

"You're the most fiercely loyal person I know," responded Jack. "You would never commit such a betrayal."

That her childhood comrade in mayhem was steadfast in his support eased the clench in his chest. So many of her former friends had abandoned her at the first whiff of trouble. "That's sweet of you—"

Jack cut her off with a low oath. "Damnation, it's not sweet, it's simply the truth." He frowned. "If I recall correctly, Father wrote me that you were engaged to Matherton."

She nodded.

"Never liked the fellow," he muttered. "A shallow, self-absorbed fribble, out for his own gain. Had I been here, I would have advised you against the match."

Her lips quirked. "And I would likely not have listened."

Jack grinned. "True. But then I would have simply gone and pummeled Matherton to a pulp to warn him off."

The arrival of tea and a hearty selection of pastries forestalled any further discussion of the subject. The housekeeper had insisted on carrying in the tray herself and went through the ritual of arranging the table with everything positioned in perfect order.

"Cook sent your favorite gingersnaps, Master Jack, along with the cakes. And she promises to have a custard tart ready for supper."

"Thank you."

"I had her add a wedge of Stilton and a slice of pigeon pie to accompany the fresh-baked bread." Peering over her spectacles, she clucked in disapproval. "Look at you, poor mite. You need some good English fare to put some flesh back on those bones. Thin as a rail, you are."

"And twice as pale—isn't that how the old nursery rhyme goes?" Kyra ducked her head to hide a smile. Even in his present state, her old friend was hardly a 'mite.'

Mrs. Ganton wagged a finger at her. "You, too, Missy. A tiny sparrow eats more than you do. When I come back, I don't want to see aught but crumbs left on this platter."

Jack snapped off a jaunty salute. "You know I never dare disobey a direct order from you, Ganny."

"Hmmph." The housekeeper tried to maintain a stern expression, but as she moved through the blade of sunlight, the glitter of wetness in her eyes softened the effect. "And pigs may fly."

"Speaking of gammon, I would welcome a platter of Cook's special spiced ham for supper."

"I shall pass on the request," answered Mrs. Ganton. "No doubt she will cosset you with any delicacy your heart desires."

"Spare the rod, spoil the child—isn't that an old English adage?"

Kyra looked around to find Rafael leaning against the fluted moldings of the doorway. His face was angled in such a way as to hide all but the upward curl of his mouth.

"Indeed," replied Jack cheerfully. "A fact that was drummed into me often enough in my misspent youth. The slap of the birch on my bum left a lasting impression!"

"Oh, fustian," she said. "As if your father ever resorted to corporal punishment, much as you deserved it."

"Well, I might be guilty of a slight exaggeration—but I'm sure Cook took a cooking spoon to my bottom when I filched a handful of her freshly baked gingersnaps."

Straightening from his slouch, Rafael interrupted the banter by clearing his throat. "Speaking of your father, Jack . . ." He stepped back to reveal the earl's frail figure hovering in the shadows.

Hendrie took a tentative step forward. "Dear God in Heaven. D-Dare I believe it is really you?"

Jack levered to his feet, and in the flickers of sunlight dancing in through the windows, she saw a spasm of emotions ripple beneath his usual sardonic smile.

"Halloo, Father. Yes, I'm afraid you are stuck with me for a little while longer. Like a cocklebur, I seem to be a stubbornly difficult entity to dislodge from this mortal world."

Hendrie drew in a lungful of air and let it out in a wordless sigh.

The sound seemed to break the awkward silence. Both father

and son moved at once and in a heartbeat were in each other's arms.

Kyra quietly rose and went to join Rafael in the doorway, not wanting to intrude on the intimacy of the moment.

"I seem to have turned into a watering pot this afternoon," sniffed the earl when at last he broke off his embrace and began to search his pockets for a handkerchief.

Jack's eyes were none too dry either, she noted. "Would you care to join us for some tea, sir? I will ring—"

"To the devil with tea," said Rafael. "I think the occasion calls for a bottle of champagne."

A LOUD POP, a cheerful fizz. Rafael watched the sparkling wine bubble up in the crystal glasses, the effervescence swirling with the soft laughter to create a simple symphony of joy.

As Hendrie poured the libations, Jack was recounting the details of his ordeal—the slow recovery of his consciousness, the difficult retreat through Spain to French territory, the kind French officer who had befriended him and helped arrange his freedom and, finally, passage back to England. Rafael knew from his own experience that there was a darker side to the story that his cousin was holding back.

The fetid field hospitals, the screams of the dying, the agony of bouncing over rutted roads

Those nightmares would linger, but he and Jack were among the lucky ones. They were alive.

Alive.

"A toast," he said, raising his glass. "To life."

"Amen to that," seconded his uncle with unabashed enthusiasm.

Kyra's reaction was harder to discern. She hesitated and

seemed to be contemplating the tempest of tiny bubbles exploding in her wine.

Which must mirror her own conflicting feelings, he mused. Her heartfelt joy at the return from the dead of her old childhood friend had to be tempered by the painful reminder of her sister's tragic accident.

There would be no miraculous resurrection.

As for her own spirit . . .

"Yes, to life," she said softly, echoing of his own sentiment. "It is precious beyond words, is it not?"

"Indeed," he agreed. Their eyes met. "Without question."

Hendrie uncorked another bottle, the happy flush on his face no doubt accentuated by a surfeit of spirits. Rafael swallowed a grin, along with another taste of the wine. They would all likely end up well foxed this afternoon, but if ever a day deserved excess celebration—

"Good Lord, Hendrie, I just heard the news from Mr. Wogdon, who says he just delivered your son to your door." Kyra's father rushed into the drawing and paused to catch his breath. "Good Lord," he repeated, catching sight of Jack "It *is* you, you young scamp!"

"In the flesh, Your Grace," replied Jack.

"Well, I'll be damned." The duke blinked and pursed his lips. "I am delighted to see you. But be forewarned that if you think you can return to your habit of galloping your stallion through my south orchard and trampling the young saplings, you had best think again." A sniff. "I am still capable of taking a switch to your bottom."

"I would expect no less, sir," drawled Jack.

"Have some champagne, Pierpont." Hendrie thrust a glass into his neighbor's hand. "You may breath fire and brimstone later, but for now let us have naught but jovial sentiments to celebrate the moment."

"Right-ho." The duke drained his glass in one long swallow.

"Speaking of celebrations, I think your son's return calls for a rather large one, don't you think? There are a number of neighbors and friends who will want to offer their felicitations."

"A party," mused Hendrie. "Yes, of course. That's a splendid idea. Perhaps an outdoor supper in the gardens, now that the weather is warming, with tables of punch, and fiddlers from the village to add a note of jolliness to the evening."

Rafael saw the duke slant a quick look at his daughter.

"Actually, I was thinking of more than a supper party. It seemed to me that all of Jack's friends both here and in London would love to welcome him home with something grand—like a festive ball."

"But Father . . ." whispered Kyra.

"A splendid idea," exclaimed Hendrie before she could say more. "Though the ballroom here is in the older part of the house and may be a bit cramped for a large gathering."

"Then let us hold it at Pierpont Manor! There is more than enough room for dancing, and I can easily accommodate a number of people in the east wing, so we need not worry about limiting the guest list."

"Father," Jack said, but Hendrie appeared not to hear him.

"Ah, an evening aswirl with silks and satins, and everyone dancing until dawn!" The earl was smiling from ear to ear. "It's been quiet as a crypt here for far too long. It's about time to have some laughter and revelries."

Kyra was looking pale as a ghost.

"What say you, Jack?" added the earl.

Jack drew in a measured breath. "Perhaps you are right. Perhaps a bit of laughter and revelry will do us all good."

CHAPTER 10

aughter and revelry. Try as she might, Kyra couldn't seem to shake the unsettling words from her head. Edging around the elderberry hedge, she crouched down and cut a handful of yellow-flowered sprigs from the clump of *Hypericum perforatum* growing alongside the weathered stones of the garden wall. The herb, commonly known as St John's wort, was said to lift the spirits, so perhaps she would tipple a taste of the herbal tonic she was making for elderly Mrs. Bailey, a widow who lived in a cottage bordering the estate.

After all, it was also known as "chase-devil," and if ever she need a blue-deviled mood to be banished . . .

Blowing out a sigh, she gathered another bunch of the flowering plant, then moved onto a patch of calendula. Bees flitted through the twisting vines of climbing roses that wreathed the stones, their droning buzz surprisingly soothing as she worked. A breeze ruffled through an overhanging apple tree, stirring the sweet fragrance of the pink-tinged blossoms and the flicker of diamond- bright sunbeams through the dancing leaves.

It was, mused Kyra, hard to stay dispirited amidst all the splendors of nature. The floral scents, the vibrant colors, the chirping serenade of the crickets and the cooing turtledoves in the nearby wooded glade all seemed in such harmony.

"It is selfish to brood," she chided herself, stifling a laugh as she watched Hero gambol along the wall in chase of a butterfly. Especially in light of the happiness surrounding Hendrie Hall. She had seen little of Rafael and Jack during the last week, feeling that the cousins would wish some private time together to sort through all the fierce emotions of the unexpected reunion. Both had suffered greatly during the last six months, and there were wounds both in body and spirit that needed each other's help to heal.

She had sensed that guilt over his own survival on the battlefield had left far greater scars on Rafael than the saber slash to his leg. Now, with his cousin's miraculous return, the lingering damage to his peace of mind would soon be gone. A smile played on her lips. And part of the credit would belong to Rafael's grandmother and her notes on the magical properties of cacao. His growing expertise with chocolate would be good medicine, not only for Jack, who was in need of nourishment, but also for himself.

To her eyes, the handsome Spaniard was still too thin.

Though perhaps, Kyra concededly wryly, that was the pot calling the kettle black. However, she was no longer merely skin and bones. Strangely enough, her appetite—for more than just food—had slowly returned. She watched the patterns of pale sun-warmed hues from the overhead leaves dapple the sleeves of her calico work dress. Yes, she owed some of her returning strength to the healthful qualities of Rafael's chocolate.

But the real tonic had been his friendship. He had made her feel that there had developed a bond between them—that their shared interests, their shared laughter, and their shared exploration of ideas had helped brighten his own bleak spirits.

He seemed to enjoy her company.

As I do his.

Her basket now brimming with herbs, Kyra rose and made her way to the path leading back to the manor house. Of course, if he had any inkling about the true depths of her depravity, he would be too shocked to continue the acquaintance, much less keep up the closeness that developed between them.

What he knew about her transgressions was bad enough. But he must never, *ever* guess at the fundamental flaw in her nature.

"I am unfit company for an honorable gentleman," she whispered. So no matter how much she yearned for his touch, she must keep her distance.

Hero's happy bark drew her thought back from the precipice of brooding. He bounded up with a stick in his mouth and dropped it at her feet.

"You have taken to country life as if you were to the manor born," she said dryly.

Woof.

"Yes, yes, Your Lordship. I see I am expected to cater to your whims." Picking up the length of beechwood, she hurled it over a low hedge bordering the sloping lawns that ran down to the lakeside folly. The dog took off like a pistol shot, oversized paws and plumed tail a blur of iron-gray as he vaulted over the greenery.

Shoving her black thoughts aside, Kyra decided it was wrong to dwell in self-pity with so much exuberance all around her. Life, she reminded herself, was a celebration in itself. She would try to be mindful of embracing the light instead of the dark.

The sweet, grass-scented breeze tickled her nostrils, and after a few steps she found herself simply enjoying the moment. The path turned and wound through a pergola covered with thick twines of glossy ivy. The sudden coolness of the shade sent a shiver down her spine, but in a moment she was back out into the welcome warmth of the sunlight—

"Ah, I've found you at last."

The voice caused her to freeze in her tracks.

"Still fussing with your precious herbs and flowers, I see."

Willing her heart to stop hammering against her ribs, Kyra turned slowly to meet the all-too-familiar smile.

"Lord Matherton," she said, trying to keep her voice steady.

HIS BROWS WINGED up in question as he stepped out of the jagged shadows and flicked a leaf from the sleeve of his elegant coat. "What? So formal?" The smile stretched a tad wider. "In the past, you were happy to call me Chas."

"Why are you here?" demanded Kyra tightly.

"Do I not get a more tender greeting than that? After all, we are close friends." Somehow Matherton made the words sound slightly sordid.

She was tempted to reply that close friends do not abandon close friends. But instead, she merely shifted her basket from hand to hand and repeated her question.

"You are angry with me." Her former fiancé looked up at her through his gold-tipped lashes. "I cannot say that I blame you, sweeting. And I am sorry for what happened—truly I am. But please try to understand what a precarious position I was in."

Kyra could not quite decipher the half-hidden glimmer of emotion in his eyes, however she was quite certain it was neither regret nor recrimination.

"Given the rumors, I . . . well, you have to admit that I had reasons to wonder."

"Wonder if I had shared my favors with another because I had shared them with you?" she finished for him. The rumors that had sprung up after the accident had been horribly nasty, and a part of her hadn't blamed him for crying off. And yet . . .

Matherton lifted his well-tailored shoulders. "No gentleman wishes for there to be a whiff of scandal tainting his bride."

How had she ever found him seductive? At the present

moment, his self-serving smugness slithered across her skin like a serpent, stirring naught but an unpleasant sensation.

"So I ask again, why are you here?"

"Because I've realized how much I adore you." Another smile. "And how wrong I was to let you go."

It might have been a sentiment to make a lady's heart melt had it not sounded so rehearsed.

"We both made mistakes, my lord. Let us leave them in the past." Kyra turned to walk away.

"Wait." He caught hold of her arm. "You can't mean that. Not after what we had between us."

"Oh, but I do," she replied calmly. Had it only been six months ago when she had been besotted with his handsome face, his intimate smiles? Strange how it felt like a century. She was such a different person now. *Older, wiser, her youthful hubris tempered by adversity.*

"I see now that we never would have suited," she went on. "What we had was not as meaningful as it should have been. Had the bond been truly strong, it would have survived the challenge."

Matherton stepped closer, close enough for her to feel the warmth of his breath against her cheek. "Ah, I understand, sweeting. You wish for me to woo you again, to make up for my regrettable absence." The heat of him was now making her flesh prickle. "I shall be happy to do so."

"You misinterpret my meaning, sir." Kyra eased back, trying to free herself from his grasp. "So let me be blunt—I have no interest in renewing any courtship with you. There is no real love between us."

His smile thinned to a petulant scowl. "Don't play the innocent, Kyra. You know as well as I do that love has nothing to do with aristocratic matches. It's all about practical things like power and prestige." His hand tightened around her arm. "You wish to be blunt—so be it. I'm willing to restore you to respectability and in return I become the Duke of Pierpont's son-in-law, a position that will be of great benefit to me."

"And of course there is my very generous dowry, which will also be of great benefit to you."

"It seems to me to be a fair exchange," answered Matherton.

"Perhaps it is. But I am not interested."

His face darkened, anger casting a shadow over the handsome features. "Still the same spoiled, willful chit as before, I see. But I think you will change your mind soon enough once you've heard the rest of what I have to say."

Kyra had no intention of listening to another ugly word. "Please unhand me, sir. There's nothing you could say that would convince me to accept your offer."

"You would walk away and let your beloved sister's name be dragged through the mud? And ruin your father's hope of being invited to join the Royal Historical Society?"

Kyra froze, her blood suddenly turning to ice in her veins. "What do you mean?" she demanded. "Lexy was a paragon of propriety. There is nothing anyone can say that would sully her name."

"Rumors have the power to sully a saint." His mouth curled up at the corners. "Think of it, sweeting. Yet another daughter besmirched. Do you think the Duke of Pierpont would live that down? So, much as he desires to join their august group, I doubt the members of the Society would ever offer him an invitation."

"Who would do such an evil thing . . ." she began, but on catching the malicious gleam in his eye, the rest of her question died on her tongue as the awful truth suddenly dawned on her.

"*You.*" Her voice was barely a whisper. "It was *you* who started the other rumors."

"Yes, it was me," answered Matherton.

"But why?"

"Because your injuries made it uncertain as to when a wedding could take place," he answered. "And then, I was introduced to the daughter of a nabob recently returned from India. Granted, there was no prestigious title attached to the family name, but the chit had a far bigger dowry than you did. I needed a reason to cry off from the engagement that didn't cast me in a bad light."

His lips pursed. "But the damnable girl proved surprisingly stubborn. And then her Father hared off with the family to visit relatives in Scotland, which left me in a deucedly difficult position. You see, I am in dire need of funds. But then, as luck would have it, I heard from Lady Leverett that she had seen you at Kew Gardens, looking much like your old self."

"And you call yourself a gentleman," Kyra whispered.

He laughed, and the sound seemed to leach all the life from the colors of the gardens. "Only brainless fribbles feel bound by such antiquated notions as honor."

A wave of revulsion shuddered through her. But however loathsome she found his proposal, did she have the heart to subject her father to more pain and disappointment? It wasn't as if she could dream of a future filled with love and happiness.

"So let us not blather on about morality. I am offering you a bargain—"

"No, you are offering me blackmail," corrected Kyra.

"Call what you will," snapped Matherton. "We both will benefit." His patience seemed to be slipping away for he gave her a nasty little shake as he spoke. "What's your answer?"

"I . . ." Her throat tightened. *Yes or no?*

A sudden growl sounded. Hero bounded through the pergola, dropped his stick and bared his teeth.

Matherton let go of her and backed up a step. Though the dog was still hardly more than a pup, he had put on enough bulk to appear formidable, especially with his ears laid back and his hackles raised.

The growl sounded again as Hero came closer. Kyra had never seen her sweet-tempered dog look so fierce.

"Get away, you flea-benighted cur."

Matherton lashed out a kick, but Hero was too quick. Dodging the boot, the dog twisted and snapped his jaws, catching the cuff of his attacker's trousers.

Rip.

An oath rent the air as Matherton shook free and stared down at the tear in the expensive fabric. "Bloody Hellhound," he added, as Hero danced out of reach and snarled back at him.

"I'm warning you, Kyra. Don't trifle with me. I need—"

"Ah, are we having a bit of sporting play with the dog?"

Kyra felt a rush of relief as Jack walked out from the shadows of the ivy-twined pergola, followed by Rafael.

Jack paused to lean down and pick up the stick Hero had dropped. "Might we be allowed to join in?"

SOME SORT of game was afoot, noted Rafael as he moved with deliberate slowness across the lawn. But it was not a lighthearted one. Kyra's face was ashen, and she nearly stumbled in her haste to turn away from the handsome stranger and rush to greet her childhood friend.

"Halloo, *amigo*," he called out, as Hero bounded up, tail wagging, and licked his hand. After ruffling his fingers through the dog's coarse, curling gray fur, Rafael added, "You are a very excellent companion to your mistress, and shall have a special beefsteak treat when next you visit the Hall."

While he spoke, his gaze remained locked on Kyra. Whatever private conversation had been taking place between her and the stranger, it had left her shaken.

The gentleman's identity was quickly revealed by Jack's next words. After tossing the stick for Hero, his cousin shifted his stance and fixed the fellow with a coolly apprising stare. "What brings you out from London, Matherton? Country pursuits are not your usual pleasure, as I recall."

Matherton. Rafael felt his jaw tighten. So, this was Kyra's former fiancé. He, too, wondered what the devil the man was doing here.

"To begin with, I wished to be one of the first of your friends to welcome you back from the grave," said Matherton smoothly. "I was absolutely elated to hear of your survival."

Jack's expression turned a touch sardonic.

"As for enjoying a sojourn to the country . . ." Matherton cast a sidelong glance at Kyra. "I find it has its own unique charm."

She seemed to shrink from the ice-blue glitter of his gaze.

"And, of course, I had heard about the gala ball to be given in honor of your homecoming, and naturally I wished to be part of the festivities. Indeed, Kyra was just inviting me to attend, isn't that so, my dear."

"Yes." There was barely any breath behind her response.

"So although I must return to Town to attend to some matters, I shall be returning here again quite soon," finished Matherton.

"Be sure to bring a large trunk of clothing with you," quipped Jack. "Country life appears be a trifle rough on your usual sartorial splendor." His brows waggled as he regarded the ripped trousers. "Dear me, those look to be tailored by Weston. Does he still charge an exorbitant price for his handiwork?"

A small flicker of annoyance pulled at Matherton's smile. "That dog is wild and a menace to polite company. It could do with a good beating to teach it some manners."

"Whips and cudgels teach nothing but hate and resentment." Rafael couldn't keep from speaking up. "Earn a dog's respect and it will gladly obey you."

Anger flared in the other man's eyes, though he kept his smile frozen in place. "I didn't know you had hired a new kennel master here at Pierpont Manor, Kyra."

Jack responded before she could muster a reply. "I don't believe you have met my cousin, who prefers to go by his English name, Mr. Greeley, rather than his Spanish title of Count Olivito." To Rafael, he said, "Allow me to introduce Lord Matherton, who is a baron—or is it baronet? "

Jack's subtle emphasis on his modest title turned Matherton's expression even more hostile. "A count, eh?" he sneered. "How very impressive. However, from what I've heard, in Spain, unlike England, even base-born paupers can purchase a title."

"I wouldn't know about such things," said Rafael. His august lineage wasn't something he chose to wave around in public like a gold-threaded banner, but in this case, he made an exception. "My family is one of the oldest Grandees of Spain."

"Which is the highest and most aristocratic of all the nobility," said Jack.

Matherton merely glowered and then inclined a small bow to Kyra. "I can't tell you what pleasure it gives me to find you looking so well. I must be taking my leave. However, I look forward to seeing you again very soon. We have so much to discuss, both about the past and the future."

He started to turn away, and then paused. "Oh, and did I mention that I shall be coming with Chesterfield. We'll be staying at his family's estate in order to attend the ball. As you recall, he was a very close friend of your sister. He's been asking about you and will delighted to hear of your recovery."

Rafael didn't miss the fact that if anything, Kyra turned even paler. Her face was now as white and lifeless as the carved marble statuary decorating the nearby fountain.

Bowing her head, she stood fussing with the cut greenery and flowers in her basket until the crunch of Matherton's footsteps on the graveled path died away. "I had best be going, too. These herbs need to put away properly in the stillroom."

Rafael gave a low whistle for Hero, who had been sitting across from the pergola, the watching the proceeding while gnawing on his stick. "*Amigo*, go keep milady company as she walks to the house." A quick hand signal punctuated the command.

The dog bounded over and nuzzled her hand.

"If your Father has need of a kennel master, perhaps he should consider hiring Rafael," Jack suggested.

Kyra essayed a weak smile. "Mr. Greeley has an excellent rapport with all fauna and flora." She hesitated. "I would invite you to come in for tea . . ." Another little nervous touch to the greenery. "However, I really should attend to these."

"But of course," said Jack heartily. "We had no intention of interrupting you. We were merely enjoying a constitutional stroll along the lake and thought we would head home by way of the upper pathway."

"The walking is doing both of you a world of good. You are looking very well."

Unfortunately, the same could not be said of her, observed Rafael. She looked ready to swoon on the spot.

"Stronger every day," Jack cocked a jaunty salute as she and Hero headed off down the side path leading to the kitchen gardens.

"Something is, how do you say it in English, havey-cavey here," Rafael said as soon as he was sure she was out of earshot.

"Aye, *very* havey-cavey," agreed his cousin.

"That fellow frightens Lady Kyra."

"I've always thought him to be a thoroughly dirty dish."

Rafael wasn't familiar with that bit of cant, but its meaning was clear enough. "Have you indeed?" He lapsed into a thoughtful silence for several long moments. "Then we shall have to discover what nefarious plans Mr. Matherton has up his sleeve." A mirthless grin. "Had they been up his trouser leg, they would have been revealed.

"Clever dog," said Jack. "But we shall have to be even cleverer to best a scoundrel at his own sordid game."

"And so we shall be," vowed Rafael. "The predator may seek to prey on a lone lady, thinking she is helpless to defend herself, but he shall soon find there are sharp teeth and claws stalking his own worthless hide."

"Your sentiments appear edged with a flash of fire." A hint of a smile pulled at the corners of Jack's mouth. "It seems you have developed a rather warm friendship with Kyra."

He felt a flush steal to his cheekbones. "I . . . that is, you . . ." *Damnation*. This was a deucedly awkward subject. "I am aware that you have a very high regard for the lady?"

"The very *highest*," interrupted Jack. "I love her like . . ." There was a pause as he drew in a deep breath.

Rafael shifted uncomfortably from foot to foot. By every code of honor, his cousin had first claim to Kyra's affections. He would, of course, gracefully withdraw . . .

"Like a *brother*," finished Jack, a twinkle lighting his still-sunken eyes. "You have my blessing—nay, my encouragement—to offer yourself as her two-footed Hero."

"I don't think she would accept me if I did," he mumbled. "Yes, we have come to be friends." A grimace. "At least I think we have. But she seems determined to keep me at a distance."

"Hell's bells, can you blame her?" exclaimed Jack. "She's been badly hurt by a scoundrel. It's up to you to win her trust and convince her that not all gentlemen are callous louts."

"I am not sure how."

"You've always been far too modest, my dear cuz. Trust me, I've watched women flutter around you like moths drawn to a flame."

"All those women can't hold a candle to Kyra. She is different," said Rafael softly. "Special."

"Of course she's special." Jack grinned. "She's the lady you love."

Love.

Rafael had shied away from admitting his feelings, even to

himself. But the truth was, he *did* love Kyra. He loved her courage, her compassion, her strength. He loved her artistic spirit, her inquisitive intelligence, her luminous beauty. He loved her smile, her laugh, her grace.

Squaring his shoulders, he stared off into the gardens, watching the subtle play of sunlight and shadow bring the textures and colors of the plantings to life. "*Si*, I love her."

"Thank God," Jack cut a flourish through the air with his cane. "I thought I might have to knock some sense into your thick skull, and my arm is still a trifle weak."

"But I fear—"

"No buts, no fear," counseled his cousin. "If you wish to be worthy of her, then fight for her. And vanquish her tormentor in the bargain. We are warriors, you and I. We know how to fight. And we know how to win."

CHAPTER 11

*A*fter carefully securing the latch to the stillroom door, Kyra slumped back against the age-dark oak and tried to steady the trembling of her limbs.

One impetuous error of judgment.

Tears pooled in her eyes. Which had led to an even more grievous mistake. How could she have let herself be seduced by a serpent's forked tongue? Matherton had encouraged her to be rash, to be reckless. His words still echoed against her skull—*a daring lady is deliciously alluring.*

And she had believed him. But at heart, the fault lay with her, not with him. She could have said no to temptation.

"I am wicked," Kyra whispered, a wave of self-loathing cresting up inside her. "Wicked, wicked, wicked."

One life of a loved one had already been destroyed because of her actions. Now another hung in the balance. Agreeing to Matherton's despicable proposal was a small price to pay to protect her Father's happiness. Even if it meant giving up any hope of . . .

Pressing her back hard against the planked wood, she forced herself to forget the solemn, shadowed expression on Rafael's face as he had watched her move away from her former fiancé.

He kept his feelings well-hidden, so she could only imagine what he must have been thinking.

Nothing good, that was for sure.

Which was all for the best. He deserved a lady untainted by scandal.

She touched the sprigs of St John's wort in her basket. Already the delicate flowers were beginning to wilt. An apt metaphor for her own tentative dreams, which had been nipped in the bud.

"Not that I had any right to dream that the future might hold happiness."

An insistent scratching on the other side of the door stirred her from her mordant thoughts.

Woof.

Setting her basket on the worktable, Kyra turned and released the latch. Hero's shaggy snout nosed the door open wider and a moment later his oversized paws were leaving muddy streaks on her skirts.

"Oh, you naughty hound."

Looking wholeheartedly unrepentant, he began to bat at the flounces that trimmed her hem.

She crouched down and hugged him, unsure whether she was laughing or crying as his tongue licked the salt from her cheeks.

"What a pair we are," she mumbled, scratching behind his ears. "Two outcasts, who have been a bit bruised by life."

His tail thumped the floor, beating a jolly tattoo. It was hard to stay downcast in the face of such exuberance.

"But we have each other, and you are right." She rose, reminding herself that the herbs and cuttings were there to be put to good use in making healing salves and potions for the estate tenants. "We must not allow adversity to defeat us."

～

RAFAEL FOLLOWED the duke's butler through the stately entrance hall, careful to sidestep around the trio of maids at work waxing the wainscoting. Preparations for the upcoming ball were in full swing throughout the manor house and its grounds. Servants were everywhere, a buzz of festive excitement filling the air as they went about their appointed tasks.

Kyra, however, had proved maddeningly elusive over the course of the past week. On several occasions, he had spotted her from afar on his daily walks through the estate, but she had disappeared into the greenery of the gardens, like the fairy wood-sprite of their very first encounter.

Today, he had determined to take a more direct approach. She wouldn't come to him, so he would have to take the battle to her.

She would fight him, of course. Or rather, retreat into her private world, where shadows and demons choked off the light and laughter that should be an integral part of her life.

As they turned down a side corridor, the butler cleared his throat. "If I may be so bold as to say so, sir, the viscount's return is cause for great celebration among all the servants here. Having known him since he was a young boy, we are all very fond of him." Another rumbled sound in his throat. "Despite his occasional outrageous pranks."

Rafael smiled. "I shall pass on your felicitations, Gorman. And you may rest assured that he also drove Wellington's staff to distraction at times."

This time the cough sounded more like a smothered laugh, but the butler maintained a straight face.

"No need to announce me to Lady Kyra," he added, taking two small packages from his coat pocket. "This is an informal visit. I simply wish to hand over a little something she might find amusing."

Gorman hesitated, but only for a fraction. "Very good, sir. Shall I leave you to find your own way out?"

"Please." Rafael waited for the other man's steps to recede

before he continued on to the door of her workroom. She would likely not welcome the intrusion.

He knocked and then took the liberty of opening the door a crack.

A paw pushed it opened wider and an instant later, Hero's teeth caught playful hold of his coat and tugged him into the room.

The commotion caused Kyra to turn from her easel. "M-Mister Greeley," she stammered. "I didn't expect—"

"Did Hero not tell you that he had invited me to visit?" In his experience, humor was always an excellent way to defuse an awkward situation. "He asked me to bring him some morsels of our Cook's special creamed beef stew." Crouching down, he unwrapped the oilskin packet and set it in front of the hound. "It's his favorite dish."

She tried to look stern, but a hint of a smile appeared to be hovering on her lips.

"So, I thought I would also bring a few treats for you as well." Rafael held out the other package, a pasteboard box festooned with a jade green ribbon he had chosen to match her eyes. "Assuming, of course, that you haven't lost your appetite for chocolate."

"I have missed . . . your confections," replied Kyra softly.

"I have missed . . . your assistance in the kitchen. I am all thumbs when it comes to mincing nutmeats."

That elicited a reluctant laugh. "I have a feeling that a skilled cavalry officer is quite capable of wielding a small chopping knife."

"No, no, I make quite a hash of it. Your morsels are so much more picturesque than mine."

"Fie, you are doing it too brown, sir!"

"But of course. My grandmother's chocolate recipes deserve no less." He watched her curl the satin ribbon around her fingers. "Won't you open it? I've tried a few new creations and I would value your opinion."

Kyra slowly unknotted the bow and lifted the lid.

"Oh!"

Dismay or delight? He had pushed himself to make the selection unique and different, something that would appeal to her artistic nature. But had he gone too far?

"They look far too beautiful to eat."

Rafael released his pent-up breath. "This one is filled with a special raspberry-infused buttercream," he said, pointing to one of the quartet of confections nestled inside the box. "Beside it is a praline-coated chocolate biscuit. The pastille below it is a pastille studded with crystallized ginger, and lastly you have a ball of almond paste dipped in vanilla-scented chocolate."

Her eyes widened. "I'm tempted to sketch them."

"I'd rather you ate them."

"But they are all so lovely! It is impossible to choose one over the other."

"That is a simple problem to solve. I shall choose one for you." He flexed his fingers. "First close your eyes."

Her lashes fluttered, setting off a winking of tiny sparks. The air between them seemed to crackle with heat.

"Now open your mouth."

Her lips parted hesitantly, and at that instant she had never looked so . . . kissable. It was all he could to keep from leaning in and stealing a taste of her ethereal sweetness.

I am a gentleman, he reminded himself, *not a voracious beast.*

Getting a grip on his wayward desire, Rafael gently lifted the buttercream confection. Its silky, sensuous texture was just the thing for seducing the senses. Perhaps as it melted in her mouth, it would coax her into lowering her guard.

Just enough to trust him with whatever secret was bedeviling her peace of mind. Matherton was holding some terrible threat over her head and he needed to know exactly what it was.

"Mmmm." Her blissful, sugar-scented sigh was soft as a

dancing sunbeam against his cheeks. "You are truly a magician, milord."

"Nay, just an ordinary knave who enjoys toiling in the kitchen." He broke off a morsel of the biscuit. "Now try this—doesn't the difference in textures make for a rather delicious contrast?"

Crunch, crunch. A smile blossomed on her face, and for a fleeting moment the pinch of fear was gone. "Cooking and painting have much in common," she mused.

"Both would be bland without unexpected and imaginative elements. Colors, shapes, scents, tastes—those are the sorts of things that give an artistic endeavor its own unique character."

Looking pensive, Kyra plucked the almond paste confection from the box and took a tiny nibble. "Your observations are always so thoughtful, sir. Would that I had half your wisdom."

Sensing an opening, Rafael seized the moment. "All of mine is at your service, Lady Kyra. I would be honored to be allowed to help you, in any way I can."

She swallowed hard. "I thank you. But I don't . . . that is, I have no need—"

"Let us not prevaricate." He interrupted her stammering by lightly brushing a chocolate crumb from her lower lip. "We are friends, and friends should trust each other enough to share their troubles."

Her eyes squeezed shut.

"It's clear that Lord Matherton upset you. I would like nothing more than to counter whatever mischief he has in mind, but to do so you must tell me what it is."

"I . . . I . . ." Her voice had a hollowness that made his heart ache. "I can't."

"Why not?" he asked gently.

Kyra shook her head.

If Matherton had been within reach, Rafael would have pummeled him to a pulp for bringing such a look of utter desolation to her lovely face. He placed the box with the one remaining chocolate confection on her worktable and was about to turn and withdraw when he recalled Jack's exhortation to fight for the lady he loved.

Be damned with being a proper gentleman and allowing her yet again to retreat into the dark solitude of her private fears.

In two short strides, he closed the gap between them. "Sorry." His hands set on her trembling shoulders. "But whether you like it or not, you are not alone and defenseless against that scoundrel."

Woof!

Hero leapt up and began circling them, his tail waving in the air like a battle pennant.

"Whatever hold he has on you, I will see that it's broken," went on Rafael. "On that, I give you my promise."

Her eyes widened, and for an instant hope flared in their jewel-dark depths. Just as quickly it died away. "You far more kind than I deserve, sir," she whispered. "But I fear it is beyond your power."

He tightened his grip and pulled her close—close enough that his lips caught hers in a hard, possessive kiss for one exquisite instant before he leaned back. "No, it's not, *querida*. Men like Matherton are cowards at heart. Trust me, he doesn't stand a chance."

"I wish I dared to believe that."

"Believe it," he said decisively.

She didn't respond.

Deciding that it was time for a strategic retreat, in order to let her think about what he had said, Rafael released his hold. "I won't press you anymore today to know his threat, but please think on what I have said—sharing it with me takes away his power over you."

Hero growled and licked at her hand.

"In the meantime, you have a second loyal guardian to keep

watch over you. So come, dry your lovely eyes. You will soon be free of fear, and all the other torments that bedevil you."

"How can you say that?" asked Kyra. "You can't possibly know what I am thinking or feeling."

"But of course I can. I, too, have been to Hell and back again," he answered as he paused on the doorway. "What I learned along the way was that if you forgive yourself, your feet suddenly sprout wings, and you fly high above the smoking fires and brimstone of despair."

ree—did she dare believe him?

Lifting her skirts, Kyra climbed over the stile and picked her way down to the country lane leading into the village. She had fled her workroom, too agitated to continue painting, and decided to seek solace in the mundane task of visiting the local apothecary in order to purchase some needed supplies. The fresh scent of the meadow grasses and cheerful birdsongs that riffled through the back pastures were always calming.

Looking up at the clouds scudding across the sky, she drew in a lungful of the sun-warmed air. Free of fear? Free of recrimination? Free of self-torment? Oh, surely it couldn't be as easy as Rafael described.

He didn't know the full depths of her depravity.

A playful bark from Hero, who was thrashing through the brambles, merrily chasing butterflies, reminded her that she had vowed to put aside her worries for the moment.

"Come, Hero," she called. "Let us not dawdle." Mr. Rawlings was wont to shut up his shop early if the spirit moved him and she didn't want to miss replenishing her stock of camphor.

Kyra and the hound reached the lane as it climbed up a

sloping rise and swung around to pass through a glade of oaks. As she approached the trees, a lone rider emerged from the leafy shadows, moving at a sedate pace.

"Jack!" she exclaimed as she caught sight of his face. "I am surprised that Dr. Laskins has given his permission for you to be in the saddle just yet."

"He hasn't. But don't grass on me."

"As if I've ever landed you in the suds by telling tittle-tattle, no matter how richly you deserved it," she huffed.

"True. There was never a more loyal comrade-in-mayhem." Her childhood friend dismounted gingerly and waited for her to join him. "Lud, we were hellions, weren't we?"

"Those days are over," she said.

Wrapping the reins around one hand, Jack offered his arm and turned to walk with her. "One still needs to keep a little fire burning inside."

"Fire is dangerous."

"So is turning into a pile of cold gray ashes."

"That's unfair," said Kyra after several silent strides.

"Is it?" he shot back.

Stung by his words, she kicked at pebble in the road. "You don't understand."

"You suffered a terrible tragedy," he pointed out. "But that does not mean you have to give up on Life." He flicked a fallen leaf from his sleeve. "The Kyra I've always known had more bottom than that."

"It's easy for you say!" she blurted out. "I know you have suffered much, too—but your pain was honorably won! While I . . ." She bit her lip, unwilling to let her voice give way to a sob.

"Honor? Is that what you think?" he said in a low, tight voice. "We all have inner demons to live with, Kyra. That day on the battlefield . . ." He paused to inhale a ragged breath. "The truth is, I was a coward that day. I saw the French hussars attack Rafael, and I hesitated."

He looked away, the canopy of leaves casting dagger-like shadows over his still-gaunt profile. "Here was the cousin who was like an older brother to me. During my summers in Spain, he had taught me how to ride, how to fence, how to drink port. And in his moment of need, I was afraid—afraid for my own worthless hide."

Pain came in many guises.

She reached for his hand and twined her fingers with his.

"It was the flash of steel that roused me, I suppose," he went on. "I saw a sword rise and then start to swing down, and in that instant I managed to move. Then everything became a blur. There was blood and sweat and smoke everywhere. I saw him fall, and as I tried to reach forward, I felt a jarring pain in my chest, as if I'd been smacked with a cricket bat. That's all I remember . . . until much later."

A bleak smile flickered on his lips. "So you see, you are not alone in feeling guilty. The French hussars who found me informed me that no other English officers had survived, and so I knew that my cousin had died because I had been too selfish, too weak to save him. For weeks after I woke, I had no desire to live."

"But somehow you found the inner strength to survive." Her words were half statement, half question.

"Only because of the kindness of a French hussar's wife. She tended to my wounds, and made me talk about my childhood, and all the good memories of my family, my friendships, the estate lands that I cherished." Jack blew out another breath. "It was she who made me understand that I owed it to Rafael to live, to do my very best at fulfilling my dreams in honor of all the things he would never have a chance to do."

Kyra bowed her head, feeling a little ashamed of herself. "You must think me a willful, spoiled chit," she said in a small voice.

"I think you the same strong, courageous, wonderful hellion you've always been," he replied. "All I'm saying is that if I can come back from the dead, so can you. You just have to believe in yourself."

In his tactful way, Rafael had implied much the same thing, she mused. It sounded so simple, as yet . . .

"What you are suggesting is easier said than done."

"True. But most things worth having take struggle and sacrifice. You have weathered the hardest part of the journey, and have learned the most difficult lessons. The rest is, well, up to you." Jack released her hand, and drew his stallion close. Thrusting a boot in the stirrup, he pulled himself into the saddle. "I shall leave you to your peregrinations, for I find myself growing a trifle fatigued. The spirit may be willing to ride neck and leather through the hills as we did in our youth. But alas, the flesh is not yet up to the challenge."

"You are making great progress," said Kyra, noting that his coat no longer looked like it was hung over a bundle of sticks.

He winked. "I can say the same for you."

"I—"

"Oh, and one last thing. I wouldn't give my childhood sweetheart to just anyone. I would have come back from the grave to chase off Matherton. Rafael, however, is the best of men. He is worthy of you—and you of him." With that, Jack touched his heels to the stallion's flanks and trotted off.

The leafy shadows flickered in the breeze as the sun ducked in and out of the scudding clouds, the ever-changing hues adding their own reminder that life was rarely painted in stark shades of black and white. Lost in thought, she made no move to be on her way until Hero gave a small whine and pushed his nose against her still-curled fingers.

"Yes, yes, you are right. We ought not dawdle. Mr. Rawlings will be shutting up his shop shortly."

But despite hurrying her steps, Kyra found her thoughts straying far from apothecaries and medicines for the rest of the walk into the village. She passed the butcher shop, nearly tripping over a crate of chickens, and was about to turn down a side lane when a tentative hail brought her back to the moment.

"Forgive me, but aren't you Lady Kyra Sterling?"

She turned warily, wondering what subtle snub or snide comment might come next. The voice, soft and with a hint of an Oxfordshire accent, sounded vaguely familiar. But so-called friends had quickly sided with Polite Society in savaging her name.

"I met you at the beginning of last Season," went on the young lady. "Though I doubt you would remember me. I was one of those painfully shy girls who end up clustered against the back wall of the ballroom, like a forgotten flower left to wilt."

Kyra shifted just enough to see beneath the brim of the young lady's chip straw bonnet. Chestnut curls framed a heart-shaped face dominated by a long nose and pert mouth, which was just now forming a hesitant smile.

"You were very kind to me."

Miss Harriet Farnum. The name came to her after a moment. She was the eldest daughter of a baronet who served as a senior diplomat in the Foreign Ministry.

"I *do* remember, Miss Farnum. You had just returned to London from Stockholm, where your father had spent six months heading negotiations with the Swedish king on the war efforts," said Kyra.

Harriet's smile grew more pronounced. "I felt like a nobody, and didn't know a soul. You took the trouble to introduce me to several of the other ladies making their come-out."

"I daresay any number of people would have done the same."

"You were the only belle of London who deigned to speak to a stranger." Harriet paused. "I am staying at Grantley Manor with my good friend Lady Theodora Bingham—an acquaintance made because of you—as we've both been invited by her aunt to the celebration ball for Lord Leete. I was hoping to have an opportunity to see you and thank you for your thoughtfulness, so please forgive my forwardness in accosting you today. I wanted to seize the chance, in case it didn't come again."

Frankness deserved frankness, decided Kyra. "That's very considerate of you, Miss Farnum, however you may want to reconsider any public acknowledgement of me in the future. These days, I am a pariah in Society, and any association will not reflect well on you." Careful to keep the bitterness out of her voice, she added, "And as you know, a lady can't be too careful in guarding her reputation."

"To the Devil with my reputation," replied Harriet softly. "Let the hypocrites say what they will. I've always been taught that an honorable person values friendship and loyalty above spiteful gossip."

Kyra needed a moment to swallow the small lump that had formed in her throat. "Miss Farnum—"

"Oh, please, won't you call me Harriet? I should like to think of us as friends, that is, if you don't mind."

"I don't mind at all. Indeed I would be honored."

"Then it's settled!" exclaimed Harriet. A shop door opened and closed, setting off the tinkling of a bell and flutter of sprigged muslin. "And here is Theo, who I know would love to make your acquaintance. I'm being presumptuous, I know, but she shares your interest in the art of watercolors, and I think you would like her."

Overwhelmed by her new friend's enthusiasm, Kyra found herself swept into another round of introductions.

Lady Theodora Bingham was rather stout and plain, but she made up for her unremarkable features with a radiant smile that kindled a glint of gold in her brown eyes. "I have heard so much about your lovely paintings from my cousin, who is a member of the Royal Academy," she remarked, once the formalities were over. "Might Harriet and I be permitted to call on you soon, in hope that we might be permitted to see some of your work?"

Harriet grinned. "As you see, we are bold as brass, so we

wouldn't fit very well within the strictures of Polite Society even if we wanted to."

A bemused laugh slipped from Kyra's lips. "Well, it seems we are three peas in a pod. Or four," she quickly amended as Hero came bounding back from his exploration of empty barrels by the butcher's back door.

"Oh, what a delightful dog!" said Theo as the hound, wagging his plumed tail, tugged at the knotted cords of her reticule.

"Behave yourself, Hero," scolded Kyra, then lifted her shoulders in apology. "Please forgive his manners. He grew up in the stews of Seven Dials so we are still working on polishing off the rough edges."

"Sir Hero of Seven Dials?" Harriet tickled her fingers through the shaggy fur beneath his muzzle, eliciting a happy little woof. "I daresay there is a very interesting story to the name."

Thinking of Rafael and their wild chase through the seedy alleys near Covent Garden brought a rueful smile to her face. "It was definitely quite an adventure."

"Which we look forward to hearing when we come for a visit to Pierpont Manor," said Theo. "Would tomorrow suit you?"

"I . . . well, er . . ." Before she quite knew how it had happened, plans were quickly arranged for a tour through the estate rose and herb gardens, followed by tea.

"How lovely to have made your acquaintance, Lady Kyra," finished Theo. "Alas, I see my uncle's carriage approaching to fetch us, so we must be taking our leave."

Harriet added her farewells and the two of them hurried off.

As she watched her new friends go, Kyra blew out her breath and tried to sort out the pelter of emotions bubbling through her brain.

"Lud, what a day," she said to Hero. The last few hours had turned her carefully constructed little world helter-pelter. Inside its make-believe walls she had felt a modicum of safety.

And though Matherton had shown that was merely an illusion, it had still felt like her only place of refuge. But now, Rafael and Jack were both urging her to embrace life instead of hiding from it, despite the risk of pain.

Her gaze shifted back to the side lane, where the elderly apothecary was just stepping out to lock up his shop.

Perhaps this short trek to town was the start of a whole new journey.

~

"THIS IS GOING to be a difficult battle," muttered Rafael to himself as he passed through the entrance hall of his uncle's manor house and sought refuge in one of the quiet study rooms adjoining the library. Stripping off his coat, he went to the sideboard and poured himself a glass of Spanish brandy.

"They usually are when the stakes are high." Jack's voice floated up from behind the tufted back of the sofa set by the hearth. "And what could be more important than love?"

"Kindly stubble your sarcasm," he growled. At the moment he wasn't in the mood for his cousin's needling humor.

Straightening from his slouch, Jack ran a hand through his unruly hair. "Sarcasm?" He contrived to sound wounded. "Not at all. In fact, I rather envy you . . . even though I'm told that a tender heart is a cursed nuisance."

"Have you never been pierced by Cupid's arrow?"

A hint of hesitation, then Jack laughed. "My hide is far too thick, thank God."

"Ah, 'Methinks the man protests too much'—isn't that how your English Bard puts it?"

"Don't misquote Shakespeare," retorted his cousin.

Interesting. Despite Jack's show of bravado, it seemed that his so-called thick hide was proving surprising sensitive on the subject. However, he decided not to probe any deeper. At least for the moment.

After a quick swallow of spirits, he took a seat next to his cousin and stretched out his legs toward the brass fender. "Remember, I did attend Oxford for a term, and as I actually applied myself to my lessons, my knowledge of his plays is probably far better than yours."

"Probably." Jack raised his own glass and stared moodily at the dregs. "All that flummery and histrionics about love made my head ache."

Rafael sipped in silence for an interlude. "Who is the lucky lady?"

A grunt was the only reply.

"I take it that was a request to refill your glass."

That drew a bark of laughter. "Why not simply bring me the bottle."

"That bad, eh?"

"It's *your* romance we're concerned with at present, not mine." He drained off the last of his brandy. "Assuming I have one."

"I shall refrain from further barbs," said Rafael, after rising and pouring them each a fresh measure of the amber spirits. "Though given the merciless teasing you've given our friends over the years, I'm not sure you deserve it."

"Actually I do. I had an encounter with Lady Kyra this afternoon, and along with giving her some brotherly advice on life, I put in a good word for you, though I'm not sure *you* deserve it."

"Touché."

Jack was in a strange mood, for after his usual sardonic chuckle, he turned pensive. "The truth is, you more than deserve it. You are kind, principled, generous, strong, and a source of steady support for your family and friends. You'll make an exemplary husband."

Rafael raised a brow. "Implying you won't?"

"You know my temperament. I'm the opposite. Headstrong. Rash. Impulsive." A pause. "Selfish." Jack made a face. "Always have been."

"On the contrary, on the battlefield I saw a calm commander of his men, a brave, resourceful leader who had the courage to make the most difficult decisions under fire."

A spasm of surprise flitted over Jack's features. In a low voice he replied. "Nay, I was a coward, Rafe. At the moment of reckoning, I held back, too afraid for my own life to risk coming to your aid. God knows, I'm ashamed of myself, but I can't keep silent any longer. You must know the truth about what a weak-willed, lily-livered knave I really am." A harsh sigh rent the air as he raked a hand through his hair. "I don't deserve your good opinion."

Shock momentarily had Rafael tongue-tied. When finally he reordered his wits, he set aside his glass and steepled his fingers. "Damnation, Jack you are a man made of flesh and blood, not an automaton fashioned of brass gears and steel plates. In the chaos and confusion of fighting, with smoke stinging your eyes and screams piercing your ears, it is impossible to think rationally, or have any clear recollection of your actions."

Rafael closed his eyes for an instant, recalling the heat, the noise, the smells, and most of all, the fear. Gritty as gunpowder, it had hung heavy as a shroud in the air, distorting all normal perceptions. "You think you hesitated? For how long would you say?"

Jack's brow furrowed in fierce concentration. "At least a minute. Maybe two."

"It was no more than a blink of an eye," he shot back. "I turned just as you flung yourself down from your horse to come to my aid. You paused only to wipe the blood from your eyes, and then I saw it all happen as if it were moving as slowly as a minuet. You charged forward, heedless of the slashing steel. At that same moment, an enemy blade sliced across my thigh, knocking me to my knees. Stunned and helpless, I looked up and saw a saber rise and knew in the next instant that my life was over."

Rafael locked eyes with his cousin, refusing to let him flinch away. "But like a whirling dervish, you flew past a pair of hussars and knocked my attacker off balance. The saber blow meant for me caught you square in the chest. I tried to rise, but a musket butt smashed against my skull and everything went black. When I awoke, I was in a hospital tent, and you . . . I was informed you were dead."

Jack's face had gone deathly pale.

"So if anyone is a coward, it is I."

"Y-you're mistaken," said his cousin. "I am certain . . ." He pressed his fingertips to his temples. "That is, almost certain."

"You've always been too hard on yourself, cuz."

"Trying to measure up to you is no easy task," came the whispered response.

"*Dios Madre.*" He chuffed a wry laugh. "And here I wished I could be more like you, with your outgoing, easy manner and the ease with which you made friends."

Jack added his own gruff chuckle. "This is, you know, a very un-English conversation. Gentlemen are expected to keep a stiff upper lip."

"Yes, well I am half-Spanish, and we are known for our hot-blooded emotions. Alas, my weakness may have inadvertently rubbed off on you."

Jack took a long swallow of his brandy.

"But perhaps we should agree to stop talking about weaknesses or strengths and simply accept—and celebrate—who we are."

"Another very un-English suggestion. We are supposed to strive for perfection."

Rafael swore a cheerful oath. "What nonsense! Perfection doesn't exist. It's far better to strive for demanding the best of yourself. I have come to believe that is enough."

"Hmmm." Jack spun his glass between his fingers, setting off a cut crystal winking of gold and gray sparks against the far wall.

"Then let us leave the past behind and drink to being better men in the future."

"*Salud.*" The burn of the brandy took on a more mellow fire. "It is good that we have slain our own inner dragons, but now we must turn our efforts to helping Lady Kyra."

"As to that, I was able to enlist some unexpected help this afternoon in the village," said Jack. "I encountered an old friend, Miss Harriet Farnum, whom I've known for ages since I attended Eton with her older brother. Her father is a well-respected senior diplomat with the Foreign Office, and because of her travels, Harriet is very intelligent and independent-minded. Not only that, she remembered Kyra as being exceedingly kind to her during her first Season. So she and her companion, who are spending a month at Northfield Grange, were quick to offer their assistance when I hinted that Kyra was in need of moral support during the upcoming ball."

"Friends are a powerful influence," mused Rafael. "It gives you strength to know you are not alone."

"Precisely," replied Jack. "With all of us marshaling our efforts, Matherton is in for a rude awakening if he thinks he can intimidate Kyra into acquiescing to whatever havey-cavey plan he has in mind."

"Indeed he is." Rafael slowly clenched his hand into a fist. "Up to now, she has been on the defensive, but as we have learned from our military experience, the best time to take the offensive is when an enemy has grown overconfident that he holds the advantage."

He stared out the diamond-paned windows, giving the situation careful consideration. If only he could convince Kyra to confide in him. Perhaps creating another batch of sensual chocolate treats would melt her reservations. A creamy concoction of buttercream and champagne filling a shell-shaped . . .

"As to a plan," said Jack after a short interlude of silence, "I have an idea."

CHAPTER 13

Although Kyra experienced a small flutter of nerves on the following afternoon as the appointed time for the visit approached, her two visitors quickly put her at ease. Both of the young ladies were very knowledgeable about plant life and the tour of the ducal gardens led to much interesting talk about various local and exotic specimens on display. By the time they finished viewing the collection of herbs and headed indoors for the promised viewing of her watercolors, Kyra felt that the initial chance acquaintance was perhaps blossoming into a real friendship.

Just a short while ago, the idea would have been unthinkable.

Harriet and Theo finished perusing the paintings in the portfolio, the soft rustling of paper drawing Kyra out of her private musings.

"You are truly a gifted artist," remarked Harriet as she carefully closed covers. "Both your drawing skills and your sense of color are sublime."

Kyra colored at the compliment. "You are being far too kind."

"She's not," assured Theo. "Harriet is always honest, sometimes brutally so."

"Which is why I'll likely never marry," said Harriet. "Gentlemen tend to turn a little green around the gills when I express my opinions."

"Not all gentlemen," Kyra said, thinking of Rafael and Jack. "But you are right. The ones who are willing to give serious thought to a lady's point of view are rarer than hen's teeth."

"Lord Leete is one of them," remarked Harriet.

"You know Jack well?" she asked, curious as to how the two of them had come to be acquainted.

"Yes, he attended Eton with my older brother and often visited during school holidays. He teased me unmercifully, but I returned the favor and so we became good friends."

"That sounds like Jack," said Kyra dryly.

"You have known him for a long time as well, I take it?" asked Harriet.

"Since childhood. We shared a number of escapades and got into quite a bit of mischief together." She made a face. "I fear we were incorrigible hellions."

"What fun is life without making a little mischief," said Harriet.

Theo repressed a chortle. "Oh dear, don't remind me of Lady Sherwood's Venetian breakfast and the curry in her punch bowl."

Harriet grinned. "The coughing and sputtering made it sound like the gardens had been invaded by an army of bullfrogs."

"We would have been banned for life from the mansions of Mayfair had she ever discovered that we were the culprits," added Theo.

"Yes, but it was worth the risk. The countess is insufferably vain and she had been boasting for weeks about how her special recipe was far superior to that of any other hostess in London."

Kindred spirits. The laughter and camaraderie of friends. Kyra had thought that would never, ever be part of her life again. A spark of warmth pooled deep in her chest and slowly spread outward.

"Jack and I once crept down to Lord Berkeley's wine cellar on the eve of a fancy gentlemen's Hunt Dinner he was giving and replaced several bottles of his most expensive French brandy—smuggled, mind you!—with vinegar," she recollected. "I would have given anything to see the expression on the faces of the guests."

"Dare we stay for tea?" quipped Theo.

They all laughed, and the dulcet sound seemed to add yet another thread to the bond forming between them.

"You shall be missing a rare treat if you choose to leave before the maid appears with the tray. In addition to tea, I've made some hot chocolate from a special recipe given to me by Jack's Spanish cousin, Mr. Greeley."

"Oooh, I have heard he is a *very* intriguing man," said Theo. "Talk in London is that he is a tall, dark, brooding hero straight from the pages of Lord Byron's poetry."

"Mr. Greeley may look like a raffish corsair prince, but he is all that is honorable, kind, considerate, always willing to lend a helping hand. Indeed, it was he who rescued Hero from a pack of young ruffians." Kyra hoped her cheeks were not as blazing red as they felt. "And as he is working on turning his grandmother's cooking journals and recipes into a book on the history of chocolate. He creates the most divine confections as he performs his research in the kitchens of Hendrie Hall."

"A man who likes cooking and chocolate?" remarked Harriet. "He sounds like the very paragon of perfection."

"He is very nice," answered Kyra lamely, hoping her new friend's penetrating gaze didn't cut too deeply.

"Well then, I very much look forward to meeting him." Harriet's expression gave nothing away, but a tiny twinkle seemed to dance in her grey-green eyes. "I take it he will attending the ball."

"Yes." Kyra quickly rang for the maid, hoping to change the uncomfortable subject. "As to the ball, while we wait for our refreshments, I should like to show you the sketches for the floral arrangements the head gardener and I have designed for the supper room."

~

"I AM STILL NOT certain this is the best plan of action," Rafael said as he and Jack followed the butler down the corridor.

"Trust me, it's an excellent plan. Women are often more experienced than men at intrigue and innuendo," answered his cousin.

"Kyra isn't—"

"Yes, but Harry—that is, Harriet—is. And her diplomatic experiences have made her more practical and pragmatic than most gently-bred ladies. So I am quite confident that this is a wise move. She'll be valuable ally."

Rafael couldn't hold back a skeptical scowl.

"Just remember the strategy we agreed on. After a pleasant tea time, I will ask Harriet and her friend to allow me to ride back in the carriage with them to Northfield, as I wish to catch up with my old friend. I'll explain to them that we suspect Matherton is threatening Kyra. Not only do I trust Harriet's discretion and judgment, but she seems to have a sixth sense that alerts her to trouble in the air. As we learned in war, it never hurts to have allies in all manner of guises.

"True," Rafael conceded.

"Once we've left you alone with Kyra, it's your mission to press on and win her trust. We'll guard the flanks, but it's you who must win that victory," went on Jack. "The ladies in Spain seem to think you have a very romantic soul. It's time to wield those flowery words with the same skill as you wield your saber.

"I am counting more on the box of chocolate confections I have under my arm to loosen Kyra's tongue."

His cousin flashed a grin. "All's fair in love and war."

Quickening his stride, Jack caught up to the butler, and after dismissing him with a jovial wave, pushed open the parlor door and entered the room. "I hope you ladies don't mind if we join you," he announced grandly. "My cousin and I are famished from our walk, and we were informed that refreshments are being served here."

"You both are always welcome guests," answered Kyra. "Though perhaps I should ring for an extra platter of cream tarts."

"No need," said Rafael, following at a more measured pace. "I've brought chocolate."

Harriet flicked at her skirts and patted the sofa cushion. "Well then, do come sit beside me, sir."

"How quickly my wit and charm are forgotten," exclaimed Jack in mock dismay.

"Sweet as they are, wit and charm don't hold a candle to confections," quipped Harriet. "And I have heard that these particular creations are very special, indeed."

"Alas, even I have to admit that Rafe's culinary skills cast me in the shade." Jack quickly took charge of making all the formal introductions, and then dropped into a sprawling slouch in one of the armchairs. "There, now we need not stand on ceremony."

Rafael caught Kyra's eye, and her shy smile made his heart lurch up against his ribs.

Love might stalk a man on silent, light-as-air cat's paws, but when it pounced, it hit one with the muscled force of a full-grown lion. He sat down rather quickly on the spot indicated, surprised to find that his pulse was thudding erratically.

"Kyra has been waxing poetic about you, Mr. Greeley," began Harriet.

"And your chocolate recipes," interjected Kyra hastily, a blush ridging her cheekbones.

"Dare I hope we shall be treated to a taste of them?" asked Theo.

"But of course," answered Rafael. "I am always happy to share the fruits of my labor in the kitchen with friends." He settled the box on his lap. "Though I suggest we save them for after the main refreshments."

"Anticipation makes most things sweeter," Harriet said.

Rafael immediately warmed to her pithy humor. Jack's confidence in his friend appeared well-placed. She radiated a calm strength, and he sensed she could be counted on in a crisis.

Once tea was dispensed and the plates of pastries from the duke's kitchens passed around, the conversation turned to gardens and art. His respect increased as he listened to both Harriet and Theo express thoughtful opinions. And as he watched Kyra relax and join the animated discussion, he gave silent thanks for the power of laughter and friendship.

Now, it was up to him to prove love was an even more powerful force.

Brushing the last crumbs from her fingertips, Harriet leaned back and eyed the box of chocolates expectantly. "Mr. Greeley, I think you have kept us in suspense long enough. I'm always interested in experiencing new things, and I have never tasted edible chocolate before."

Theo nodded her assent. "Nor have I. Indeed, I have never even heard of it being possible."

"I warn you, don't get Mr. Greeley started on its history unless you wish to stay for supper," teased Kyra.

"I do tend to become a prosy bore on the subject," he replied.

"Oh, not at all," she protested. "It's absolutely fascinating, but as the story begins back in the time of the Aztec Empire, it might be best to wait and make it an evening's entertainment."

"Perhaps we could gather in the kitchen and watch you cook as you regale us with its lore and legends," suggested Harriet.

Theo clapped her hands together. "What a splendid idea!"

"I agree," said Kyra. "You make it come alive."

There was a sparkling intensity to her eyes, the nuanced hues rich and vibrant, in contrast to the dull flatness of their first few meetings. Never would he allow her to be robbed of that vitality again. She deserved light and laughter, not darkness and despair.

"We shall arrange such an evening," answered Rafael. "But be forewarned that I may put you work helping to prepare the ingredients.

"Having traveled to some far more primitive places that the mansions of Mayfair, I am no stranger to cooking," replied Harriet.

"Nor am I," added Theo. "It may surprise you gentlemen, but we ladies acquire a variety of practical skills in our dealings with estate tenants."

Rafael was fast learning not to underestimate the mettle of the cosseted, sheltered daughters of the *beau monde*. The delicate frills and fluttery ribbons often hid a sharp intellect and a spine of steel.

"My grandmother was extraordinarily accomplished in a great many fields, so I assure you, I am not surprised by how capable you are." He lifted the lid from the box of chocolates. "So I propose a toast of sorts. I have fashioned these confections with a center of buttercream flavored with champagne."

Three feminine sighs sounded in unison.

"You really must teach me how to make those," quipped Jack. "It seems that a gentleman needs only chocolate to make him irresistible."

"You will need more than sugar and spices to make your sharp-tongued humor palatable to the ladies," shot back Rafael.

His cousin grinned. "I'm willing to take my chances."

"You two may trade barbs, but while you do . . ." Kyra rose and scooped up the box from his lap. "We ever-practical ladies will feast on these treats." A wink to her new friends. "We may leave you a taste if you behave."

"No promises," interjected Harriet as Kyra offered her the selection of sweets. She took one of the nut-brown balls and popped it into her mouth. Her eyes closed, and for several moments there was silence.

Rafael shifted in his seat. Perhaps the wine was not such an inspired choice after all. Had it soured—

His worries were cut short by a blissful purr.

"That," announced Harriet with a dreamy smile, "is absolutely divine."

Theo quickly helped herself to one, followed by Kyra.

"You will make some lucky lady *very* happy, sir," went on Harriet.

"Sorry." Kyra cleared her sudden sputter with a cough. "A piece of walnut caught in my throat."

"As you see, I need your help to make them just perfect." Rafael turned to the others. "Lady Kyra is a dab hand at mincing nuts."

"Lady Kyra possesses a number of exquisite talents," replied Harriet.

Two hot spots of color blossomed on Kyra's cheeks.

"She does," he said softly. "In any number of ways."

"Let us not wax too lyrical. She has her faults, as I know well." Jack took two confections and casually gobbled them down in one quick swallow. "She can be maddeningly impetuous and stubborn."

Kyra huffed an aggrieved protest.

He grinned. "But I adore her all the same."

As he reached for another chocolate, she caught his hand. "Feeding you Mr. Greeley's creations are akin to casting pearls before swine. They are meant to be savored, like fine wine or vintage brandy."

"Oh, there's an excellent idea. Next time, do try brandy, cuz. Fire is even more potent than fizz."

"I think the ladies appreciate a more subtle mix of flavors," pointed out Rafael.

"Quite likely." replied Jack. "Clearly you understand the feminine mind better than I do."

Harriet let out a low snort. "True. Otherwise you would not have eaten the last confection."

Rising, Jack made a show of flexing his lanky limbs. "On that note, perhaps it's time to take my leave. My sterling qualities seem cast in the shade by my cousin's unique talents."

"You are not without your own charms," responded Harriet, as she gathered her skirts and rose gracefully from the sofa cushions. "And we shall allow you to regale us with them during the carriage ride back to Northfield."

"Speak for yourself," said Theo. "Though I may be coaxed into forgiving you for snatching the last bit of champagne buttercream if you promise to ask me to dance at your homecoming ball. I usually spend all my time sitting with the matrons, and for once I would like to twirl across the polished parquet in the arms of a dashing gentleman."

Capable of faultless manners when he so chose, Jack swept into a gallant bow. "Consider yourself claimed for the first waltz, Lady Theodora."

"And the second," added Rafael. "That is, if you don't mind dodging my clumsy steps. I warn you, I don't dance well, so there is a good chance you'll be nursing sore toes by the time the music has ended."

Theo turned shell pink. "I did not mean to sound so encroaching, sirs! The waltzes are the highlight of the ball and should be saved—"

"For the most interesting, alluring ladies of our acquaintance," interrupted Rafael. "Please don't say no. Or we won't have the courage to ask Miss Farnum or Lady Kyra as well."

"I, um . . . yes," stammered Mary. "If you put it that way."

"Excellent! That settles it," exclaimed Jack. "The three of you must consider yourselves engaged to stand up with us, and we shall not allow you to fob us off for another of your many admirers."

"Very well," said Harriet dryly. "We shall beat them off with a stick." Turning to Rafael, she asked, "Do you wish to come along with us in the carriage?"

"No, no, my cousin has some artistic matters he wishes to discuss with Kyra," replied Jack smoothly before he could answer. "Chocolate, art . . ." A sly wink. "Poetry."

"Sounds like a very interesting conversation," Harriet said.

"So come along, ladies." A quick wave urged his two companions toward the door. "Let us be on our way." After a flurry of farewells, the trio took their leave, and in short order, the echo of their steps in the corridor faded to silence.

"Poetry?" inquired Kyra.

Rafael's face went through a series of odd little contortions. "You know Jack. He often enjoys stirring the coals and bringing the pot to a bubble."

"Ah." She couldn't resist a little teasing of her own. "So you *do* wish to talk about cooking?"

"Not really." He shifted, and the sunlight hung for a moment on his lashes, lighting the fleck of gold in his chocolate-dark eyes.

A clench of longing squeezed at her chest.

"Though I do hope you enjoyed the confections," he went on. "The idea came to me on a whim."

"Artistic inspiration often does," she replied. "They were sublime." *You are sublime, though I shouldn't dare think it, and most assuredly shouldn't dare say it.* "I do hope you wrote down the recipe."

"I did." His expression turned more serious. "As for my next words, I haven't made any notes, so they may not turn out quite as well."

Kyra waited warily for him to continue.

"The fact is, I have a favor to ask of you."

His tentative half smile, a subtle curl of his sensuous lips, made her bones feel as if they were made of butter. *Warm butter.* She looked away, trying not to let her resolve melt. "Yes?"

He closed the distance between them with two swift steps. The heat of him prickled against her skin. "I would like for you to trust me with whatever secret you are hiding."

Impossible.

"You've asked that before," she answered softly.

"And I will ask it again, and again, until you agree." He reached out and gently tilted up her chin. "I am a very stubborn fellow."

"I can't."

"You can. But you won't." His smile became more pronounced. "My English is still a little ragged, but I do know the difference between those two words."

In that instant, Kyra would have gladly journeyed to Hell and back if he had asked it of her. But this . . .

"It's too shameful," she whispered. It was one thing to confess Matherton's threat. But the heart of her former fiancé's hold over her was something more elemental, and she knew she couldn't bear to be anything less than honest with Rafael about it.

"We all do things that we regret, *querida*. There is nothing shameful in that. It simply means we are human, and far from perfect."

"The rumors are true," she blurted out. "I am a broken vessel?"

Rafael made a show of studying her face, which only made her flesh take on a hotter burn. She was sure she must be glowing scarlet—an apt hue for a wanton jade.

"How strange," he commented. "I see no cracks or chips."

"It's not a jest, sir."

"It wasn't meant as one."

She hitched in a breath, and then, having no idea how to respond, let it out in a ragged sigh.

"If you are ruined, then so am I." A glint of humor rippled through his gaze. "And, I daresay, so are a great many more people than we might imagine."

"It's different for you. Men are allowed—nay, they are expected—to sow their wild oats."

"Surely a lady as wise as you are has figured out that such self-serving blather is because it is men who have written the rules over the centuries."

Amusement welled up in her throat. "Oh, I shouldn't laugh. It's wrong. It's wicked."

"Of course you should. Humor is needed most when things are grimly serious." His arms circled her shoulders, and all at once, Kyra found herself nestled against his chest, the steady beat of his heart resonating through her whole body.

Had he kissed her, the spell might have been broken. However, Rafael simply held her close, and by some enchantment, a feeling of peace seemed to pulse through her, overwhelming all her doubts and fears.

"You are the most confusingly wonderful man in the world," she whispered against the soft melton wool of his coat. "I know that makes absolutely no sense but my whole world seems to have turned topsy-turvy of late."

"It makes perfect sense. Life is full of confusions and contradictions. It makes you ache abominably, only to fill you with joy at the most unexpected moments." He gently stroked his finger across her cheek. "We must simply do our best to keep our equilibrium through all the highs and lows."

"Even if the lows seem to plunge you into a chasm deeper and darker than the pits of Hell."

Without hesitation, Rafael answered with a firm "Yes."

Kyra slowly slid her arms around him, reveling in the feel of his lithe muscles and broad back.

"Nothing is so bleak as you describe if you do not try to face it alone," he added.

Trust. That word again, its echo rising up to taunt and torment her. Or maybe it was the demons in her head who were the tormentors. Might it truly be possible to silence them?

"You may be horrified," she said in a small voice. "You see, before I share with you the details of Matherton's demand, I must first tell you the whole truth about me."

"Never." He drew her even closer, wrapping her in his strength and support.

The words seemed to make the decision for her—they simply spilled out of their own accord. "As I told you, I'm guilty of sins of the flesh. That's shameful enough, but it is even more sordid. I enjoyed it."

His hold remained unflinchingly strong and steady. "You think that shameful?"

"Only wicked and wanton females take pleasure in such intimacies," she admitted.

"What utter fustian." He shifted, and all at once his palms were framing her face. "There is nothing more beautiful and joyful than two people sharing delight in both body and soul. Love is expressed most fully through every essence of our being."

She felt as if a ray of sunlight had suddenly pierced the iron-gray clouds shrouding her spirits.

"I assure you, *querida,* any man worth his salt would wish for his lady to equally enjoy the act of love."

"Y-you make it sound sublime, rather than sordid."

"It is," replied Rafael. "With the right person, and with all the right reasons."

"I . . ." Kyra looked up to find his lips were only a hairsbreadth away from hers. She lifted her chin.

Flesh touched flesh in a gossamer-soft kiss.

In another heartbeat . . .

Woof. Nosing open the door, Hero burst into the room, a waggling blur of shaggy fur and flailing paws. *Woof, woof.*

"Ah, here you are, my dear." The duke followed at a more dignified pace. He cleared his throat with a brusque cough. "Forgive me. I thought your guests had departed."

Jumping back with a flustered hop, Kyra tugged her skirts free of the hound's playful nips. "Mr. Greeley remained behind to give his opinion on my sketches for the flower arrangements. He is very knowledgeable about botany."

"You are a cleverer fellow than I am," said her father, directing a friendly nod at Rafael. "Can't tell a peony from a petunia."

"He can even discern the difference between the new China roses and our traditional English varieties," added Kyra, hoping her voice didn't sound too brittle.

"Just don't ask me about lilies," said Rafael dryly.

The duke laughed. "Wouldn't dream of it." After a glance at the mantel clock, he added, "The hour is growing late, sir. You are very welcome to stay for supper."

"That is most kind of you, Your Grace, but I had best be returning to Hendrie Hall."

"Shall I summon one of the carriages?"

"Please don't trouble yourself, sir. The walking does me good. I shall just let myself out through the French doors here and be on my way." He bowed to the duke, and then to her. The smile that curled on his mouth as their eyes met for an instant sent a shiver dancing down her spine.

"A rare fellow," her father said as he watched Rafael cross the terrace and descend to the graveled walkway leading down to the lake, followed by a frolicking Hero. "He seems to be a man of unusual interests."

"Indeed," she said, still savoring the all-too-fleeting kiss—and yearning for more.

As Kyra turned to retie the ribbons of her portfolio and put it away, she caught his searching look. For the first time in ages, she didn't shy away. "He is, without question, quite unique."

~

"Ungrateful mutt—you are in danger of being sent back to Seven Dials," scolded Rafael, shooting a black look at the capering hound.

On hearing the words, Hero bounded over and licked his hand.

"Oh, very well, you are forgiven." Laughing, he tweaked the plumed tail. "I suppose it's just as well the duke did not find me with his daughter in my arms. When I make my proposal, I would prefer not to be staring down the barrel of a pistol."

Lengthening his stride, he rounded the marble folly overlooking the sun-dappled lake. A light breeze ruffled through his hair, bringing with it the chirping of the crickets and the fluttery cooing of a nearby dove. Butterflies flitted through the tangle of wild roses crowning the old stone wall, setting off bright flashes of yellow and gold against the deep pinks and greens.

Life is beautiful, he thought, lifting his face to the heavens. Just months ago, the world had seemed a grimly gray place, leached of all color. Love wielded a magical brush, painting the world in a palette of hope and joy.

"Love." He whispered it softly, then shouted it aloud, laughing softly as the echo reverberated through the trees.

Hero look back and cocked his shaggy head.

"Yes, yes, I'm a besotted fool." He grinned. "But I have good reason to celebrate."

The hound gave an encouraging *woof.*

Rafael couldn't help but share his elation. "I know I can trust in your discretion, *amigo.* We are allies, you and I, in the fight to win my lady's heart. And we have achieved a great victory today. For you see, up until now, I was battling an unknown enemy.

Now that I know what I am up against, the fight becomes infinitely easier. I will of course need to know the specific threat Matherton is making. But I have every confidence that happen very soon."

That Kyra thought herself wicked and wanton for feeling desire still had him reeling. He shook his head in consternation, realizing yet again how ladies were confined within a very rigid cage of rules. A gilded cage, but a cage nonetheless. It was no wonder that anyone with imagination and curiosity felt compelled to break free of the bars.

Sympathy quickly gave way to a more primitive emotion. That she felt desire sent a clench through his own body. "Mark my words, *amigo*," he said to his companion. "I will vanquish the last of her fears and win her hand in time to dance the midnight waltz at the upcoming ball."

CHAPTER 14

Shifting her heavy reticule, Kyra climbed over the stile and hurried to the footpath leading along the perimeter of the grazing field. In the distance, sheep dotted the long meadow grasses, white flecks in the ripples of green and gold. Overhead, the scudding clouds mirrored the pastoral scene, their wispy puffs moved lazily across the sea of blue.

Her spirits, already buoyed by the beautiful morning, rose even higher as the bag bumped up against her hip. The book inside it was a serendipitous discovery, and she couldn't wait to share it with Rafael. Her emotions too unsettled for sleep, she gone down to the library in the wee hours of the morning. Books were always a calming influence, and on a whim, she had chosen to wander through one of the back alcoves that held a collection of dusty old tomes acquired by her grandfather. To her delight, one of them had turned out to be a journal from an early explorer of the New World containing copious sketches of the local flora and fauna—including *Theobroma cacao*!

Kyra smiled, imagining his expression on seeing such a treasure. His curiosity was one of the things she loved about him. Unlike most gentlemen of privilege, he was so imaginative, open to new experiences, new ideas. Not to speak of being kind, compassionate and shockingly radical in his acceptance of women as equals.

Skirting a rock outcropping, she followed the path into a glade of coppery beech trees. Shards of sunlight glittered through the canopy of leaves, diamond-bright flashes that softened the shadows. Filling her lungs with the cool, earth-scented air, she let it out with a silent shout of joy.

Love. Giddy with wonder, Kyra finally dared to believe it was possible. Rafael hadn't found her despicable or disgusting. He knew her darkest secret and still he had kissed her so sweetly, so tenderly. She touched her lips, and felt a quiver of wry laughter. Oh, if not for Hero's bark it might have turned more passionate than tender—and the idea sent a lick of fire tingling down her spine—

A low growl jerked her from her reveries.

Hackles raised, Hero was standing stiff-legged in the path. He snarled again as a figure stepped out from the trees.

"I was hoping your habits hadn't changed and I'd find you out at this ungodly hour traipsing the fields."

Matherton's voice seemed to turn the air cold as ice.

"Call off your watchdog." Her former fiancé brandished a stout, iron-tipped walking stick. "We need to talk."

She gave a soft whistle and called the hound to her side. Fisting a hand around his collar, she gave a curt nod. "Go on."

His handsome face pinched into a malevolent scowl. "Don't take that high and mighty tone with me, my dear. Have you forgotten that I can ruin your family with no more effort than this!" He snapped his fingers.

Kyra held back an angry retort. Rafael had given her the courage to believe such threats would soon cease to have any teeth. But as she had yet to explain the particulars to him, she decided to bide her time.

"I've not forgotten," she answered.

"Then I suggest you look a little more pleased to see me." He took a step closer. "After all, we're soon to be leg-shackled and for now, people must believe that our rekindled romance is a match made in Heaven."

Or rather Hell, Kyra thought.

When she didn't answer, Matherton went on, "Indeed, I've decided the perfect place for the announcement of our nuptials is at your father's ball for Leete. Resurrection and redemption—it will bring tears of joy to even the most jaded of hearts, don't you think?"

What she thought was that he was a cold, calculating monster.

With a flick of his stick, he reached out and tipped her chin. "Speechless with joy, my dear?"

Hero lunged and snapped.

Kyra managed to keep hold of his collar and drag him back, just in time to avoid the vicious blow aimed at his head.

"Oh, fie," she cried. "Only the most craven of cowards takes pleasure in hurting animals."

"Watch your tongue, Kyra," he warned, jabbing the iron point perilously close to her face. "I'll soon be the one who is holding the leash on both of you, so you ought to be trying to turn me up sweet, rather than hurling insults."

The thought made her feel a little nauseous. "Why so soon?' she asked, trying to keep her voice steady.

"Because I'm badly dipped, and my creditors are hounding me unmercifully." His eyes sparked with malevolence as they narrowed to a slitted stare. "Do as I say and you'll have a pleasant enough life. You're interesting enough in bed that it won't be a hardship to beget a brat or two on you. Rusticating at the Grange will suit your country habits, while your father's money will allow me to have a handsome townhouse in London."

Not a penny of the Pierpont coffers would ever find its way to his pockets, vowed Kyra.

"But if you try to make trouble . . ." Menacing as a cobra, the stick swung back and forth in front of her face. "Just remember, I am a dangerous man to cross."

She was saved from having to answer by a loud hail. "Halloo, Kyra!"

Thanks God. Relief flooded through her as she returned Harriet's greeting.

"A lovely morning for a walk, isn't it?" added Theo as she and Harriet hurried down the twisting path to join them.

Matherton's face underwent an utter transformation as he quickly schooled his features to assume a cherubic expression of sunny charm. "Good day, ladies. I couldn't agree more." He gave his walking stick an innocent little twirl. "There is nothing like a brisk stroll through the splendors of Nature to put a man in a good mood for the rest of the day."

"Oh? Is there something wrong with your mood this morning, Lord Matherton?" asked Harriet coolly.

A flicker of irritation marred his mask of gentlemanly virtue for just an instant, but he quickly resumed his polite smile. "If there was, it was quickly put to flight by the presence of three beautiful ladies."

Ignoring the florid compliment, she turned to Kyra. "We are just returning to Northfield by a shortcut through the orchards. Why don't you come along and join us for tea."

"That would be lovely."

"Hero is of course invited, too," said Theo as she exchanged caresses with the hound. "Isn't he a delightful dog, my lord?"

"Delightful," growled Kyra's former fiancé through gritted teeth.

Hero wagged his tail and gave Theo's hand another wet kiss.

"If you'll excuse us, sir, we ought to be going." Theo fixed him with a frosty smile that did not begin to reach her eyes. "My aunt tends to fret if we are late." A small laugh. "As if there are predators lurking in these fields and forests."

"But of course." Matherton touched a hand to the brim of his hat, but the gesture did not quite hide the petulant scowl. His expression, however, quickly changed to a sneer as he added, "Thank you for the invitation to call on you at home, Lady Kyra. I will do so without delay, for I'm quite anxious to pay my respects to your father. Indeed, it will be *delightful* to renew the reacquaintance—I've sorely missed his company."

Kyra felt the air squeezed from her lungs. Dueling with the Devil was dangerous. He wielded weapons with far more skill than she did.

Harriet linked arms with her. "Good day, sir," she said firmly, then turned for the fork in the path.

Theo took up position on the other flank, and off they marched, Kyra wryly feeling like a downy chick guarded by two mother hens. It was, she realized, a very comforting sensation.

After checking over her shoulder that Matherton had disappeared in the opposite direction, Harriet came to a sudden halt. "Sit," she ordered, gesturing to a fallen tree trunk. "You are pale as a pot of cream."

To her dismay, Kyra felt her limbs were trembling as she dutifully obeyed the order. "Sorry," she said. "I will be fine in a moment."

"Ballocks," swore Harriet. "You won't be fine until whatever threat that dastard is holding over you is rendered toothless."

"She's right," chimed in Theo. "If you tell us what is it, perhaps we can help."

Her emotions must have been more tightly wound that she realized, for Kyra all of a sudden burst into tears. "Oh, dear. I am not in the habit of turning into a water pot," she stammered in between sobs. "But I am a little overwhelmed by your kindness. I am unused to having f-friends, especially female ones."

"You had best become accustomed to it," replied Harriet dryly. "The League of Wallflowers has officially adopted you as one of their own."

"And as ladies are far wiser than men, we know that bearing a burden is made much easier by sharing its weight." Theo sat down beside her and patted her shoulder. "So as Calliope Wolcott would say—by the by, you would like Callie very much—it's time for you to spill the beans."

That turned her sniffles into a watery laugh.

"And to let us help you sort out the rotten ones and put the rest back in the jar," offered Harriet dryly. She, too, sat down.

"Would that it was so easy." Kyra sighed. "I fear that in telling you, I may be drawing you into danger. Lord Matherton is not only a very disreputable man, but he is also desperate."

"All the more reason to involve others. It will make it harder for him to implement whatever evil plans he has in mind. There is, you know an old adage that says there is strength in numbers."

She nodded thoughtfully. "As to that, I was actually on my way to Hendrie Hall." For an instant she hesitated, a little shy about revealing the reason. But her new friends had earned her unconditional trust. "To confide in Mr. Greeley. Contrary to what you think, some gentlemen do encourage sharing troubling secrets."

"He does strike me as very sensible," remarked Harriet.

"Very," agreed Theo. "He is an excellent ally. And so are we."

"I . . . I . . ."

Her two friends waited patiently while she dithered.

"I would greatly welcome your advice, if you are sure you don't mind the risk.

Harriet muttered a very unladylike word.

"You know, of course, that Lord Matherton and I were engaged. Just as you know the rumors about my ruinous behavior are true."

"And just as I can guess that it was he who seduced you," said Theo.

Kyra nodded. "Not only that, but he recently admitted that he had started the rumors in order to put an end to our engagement after the accident. Apparently he had found a richer pigeon to pluck, and as my sister's death and my own injury made it uncertain when any wedding might take place, he decided to cut his losses, so the speak, and pursue the heiress."

"I should like to cut a certain physical appendage from the dastard's worthless carcass," muttered Harriet. "It would be no loss to the ladies of England."

A chortle slipped from Theo's lips.

"Be that as it may, I assume his suit was unsuccessful," continued Harriet.

"Yes. Apparently her father got wind of Matherton's empty pockets and mounting debts, and whisked his daughter off on a prolonged sojourn to Scotland. And so, on hearing that I was recovered enough in both body and spirit to be venturing out in public again, he decided that I might be foolish enough to still harbor a tender for him." Kyra drew in a steadying breath, still ashamed of what a ninnyhammer she had been to fall for his false charm in the first place. "When I refused his offer to renew our engagement, he then resorted to blackmail."

Harriet frowned. "What sort of hold does he have over you? It is not as if he can threaten to ruin your reputation. He's already done that."

"True, there's nothing left to shred." The ironic smile quickly faded. "And so he plans on despoiling the memory of my dead sister. As he points out, two such scandals might likely send Papa into permanent decline. At the very least, it would be a horrible humiliation." She knit her hands together. "He wants very much to be invited to join the Royal Historical Society. More unpleasant rumors would likely put a dagger to that hope."

"Matherton is even more despicable than I imagined," mused Harriet. "It will make it even more satisfying to see to it that *his* reputation in Polite Society is irrevocably destroyed."

"But how—" began Kyra.

Harriet waved her to silence. "I suggest that instead of returning to Northfield for tea, we go straight to Hendrie Hall and convene a council of war with Lord Leete and Mr. Greeley. Given their military prowess, I think they will have some ideas on strategy." Her eyes narrowed in a look that might have given Matherton pause for thought had he seen it. "I, of course, have some ideas of my own, but as Newgate Prison is said to be rather uncomfortable, it might be best to come up with a more subtle attack."

~

"I TRUST that my skillful maneuvering of the troops yesterday afternoon was not all for naught." Cradling a steaming cup of spiced hot chocolate, Jack entered the library and perched a hip on Rafael's worktable. "Clearing the field for you deserves some sort of accolade." He grinned. "Or maybe a batch of your cream confections made with brandy—all for myself."

"You are becoming quite the epicurean." Rafael looked up from the page he was transcribing. "Which is quite pleasing Uncle Aubrey, so despite your sarcasm, I shall continue to feed you rich treats. He is happy to see your frame is filling out."

"I had better not acquire a taste for sweets, else I might grow *too* stout."

"That seems an unlikely danger," he replied, eying the still sharp-boned contours of his cousin's face.

"And what of the more worrisome danger?" asked Jack. "Did you manage to win any ground in the fight for Kyra's trust?"

"Yes, I did." Rafael pursed his lips. "It was a major victory, in fact, though our four-footed comrade chose an inauspicious moment to rush in to lend his support."

Jack chuckled. "Yes, I can see where *two* heroes might make things confusing to a lady."

"He did warn of her father's approach, which was fortunate, given the moment. But I do believe I've finally overcome Kyra's fears and that she is ready to confide her secret to me. Later today I plan on paying a visit?"

The butler's knock cut off the rest of his words. "Your pardon, sirs. Lady Kyra and her friends from Northfield apologize for the early hour, but wonder if you might be free to receive them?"

"By all means, show them in," responded Jack. He set down his cup and raised an inquiring brow.

Rafael shook his head, equally mystified.

They weren't left to puzzle on it for long. The trio swept in, Harriet in the lead, with Kyra and Theo close behind.

"What a pleasant surprise," greeted Jack. "May I offer you ladies tea?"

"Tea would be welcome," answered Harriet. "The three of us could use a fortifying beverage."

Kyra flashed him a quick look, but despite her tentative smile, her skin looked pale and was pulled taut over the bones of her face, making her look very fragile.

"But as you have likely guessed, this isn't really a social call, Lord Leete," finished Harriet.

"Then let us dispense with pleasantries," said Rafael, feeling a clench of alarm. "Please sit and tell what us what has precipitated this visit."

"Lord Matherton accosted Kyra this morning, while she was walking alone," said Theo as soon as they were all settled in by the hearth.

He shot from his chair with a low oath.

"In word, not deed," Harriet hastened to add.

Jack took hold of his arm. "Let us hear them out before rushing for pistols and powder.

He sat back down, still muttering invectives. "I will have his guts for garters.

"The dastard deserves no less," agreed Harriet. "But perhaps there is an even better revenge. But first . . ." She looked to Kyra.

"I was coming here to continue our discussion of yesterday, Mr. Greeley, when Matherton appeared from within the shadows of the glade," began Kyra. "He renewed his threats and demanded that I agree to announce our engagement at Jack's ball."

"Why that's only six days from now," Jack said.

She nodded. "He hasn't a feather to fly with, and needs my dowry."

"He must feel he holds a very strong bargaining chip to think you would agree to that," said Rafael softly.

Another nod. "Innuendo and scandal—Matherton wields them with rapier-like precision." She met his gaze and proceeded to explain everything.

"The depths of his depravity apparently have no bottom," he observed once she had finished.

"So we must bury him in the blackness of his own muck," said Jack. "But for that we must be as diabolically clever as he is."

"You gentlemen are far more experienced than I at warfare," ventured Harriet. "But an idea did occur to me."

Jack's lips twitched, whether in amusement or admiration, Rafael wasn't sure. "Do go on, Miss Farnum."

"Matherton is a conceited coxcomb who has woven a spider's web of lies, false charm, and deception to achieve what he wants in life. I suggest we play on his overweening pride and avarice to trap him within the silky threads of his own manipulations."

"That sounds awfully intriguing," mused Theo.

"And awfully dangerous," added Kyra quickly.

"I should like nothing better than to see the dastard destroyed by his own creation," said Jack. "But—"

"But how are you suggesting that be done?" Rafael noted that Jack now sounded genuinely curious.

"Kyra has said that Matherton disgraced her in order to seduce a richer young lady. Supposing word went out that a very wealthy heiress was staying here in the area to attend the ball. I would imagine Matherton would turn his attentions to her.

Especially if there were whispers that Lady Kyra's dowry had suffered a great reduction because of her disgrace."

"Yes, Matherton might well be interested in a plumper purse," agreed Jack. "But there are two rather gaping flaws in your plans."

"I see only one," shot back Harriet. "The heiress, of course. And I was just about to get to that." She fluffed her skirts and grinned. "My great uncle, the black sheep of the family who went to India and became a fabulously wealthy nabob, was recently killed by a cobra's bite. The will has just been read and lo and behold, it leaves his entire fortune to me."

"Do you have a great uncle in India?" asked Theo.

"Yes." Harriet smiled. "Uncle George has, by all accounts, done very well for himself, and thankfully he was hale and hearty at the time of his last correspondence. But the point is, there enough veracity to the story to attract Matherton. Kyra has indicated he's desperate. He'll be willing to take a chance."

"That may deal with one of the flaws," replied Jack. "But you still have not addressed the second one."

Harriet frowned.

"You have neglected to consider that your friends may not agree to stake you out like a helpless lamb in order to draw a vicious wolf into a trap."

"I am far from helpless, Lord Leete," came the tart reply.

"Your abilities are unquestioned," intervened Rafael. "What my cousin means is, gentlemanly scruples, however misguided, prevent us from putting you at risk."

"Maybe we should allow Harriet to finish explaining what she has in mind before we rush to a decision," suggested Theo.

"I can't in good conscience allow Lord Matherton to threaten anyone else," said Kyra. "He is the opposite of our gentlemen companions. He has absolutely no scruples, and no honor. I don't think you comprehend how truly chilling that is."

"My point is, that we will use that coldly calculating attitude as our greatest weapon against him," answered Harriet. "There will be no danger to me, save for the fact that I will want a hot bath to scrub away the taint of his sordid presence."

"Do explain what you have in mind," urged Theo.

Rafael shot a mute appeal to his cousin. But to his surprise, Jack merely crossed his arms and waited.

"Theo's aunt is having a supper party the day after tomorrow for some of her neighbors and their London guests who've come down for the ball. We've already made sure that Lord Matherton and his hosts are invited. It will be easy to mention my new turn in fortune. I don't doubt that he will seek to strike up an acquaintance. I, in turn, will encourage it."

"He's seen that we are friends," pointed out Kyra. "And you weren't overly friendly to him this morning."

"That will play in our favor," answered Harriet. "A man of his vanity believes he is irresistible to women. That his charm can melt my reserve is something that he will take for granted."

Because of his war experiences, Rafael thought himself well-versed in human nature, but apparently the political world taught its own worldly lessons.

As if sensing his thoughts, Jack said, "I hesitate to ask how you know the foibles of such reprobate rogues."

"A diplomat's daughter meets all sorts of men," replied Harriet simply. "Many of them aren't very admirable."

"Let us grant that you will have no trouble attracting Matherton's interest. Then what?" asked Rafael as he glanced at Kyra. "He's pressing to have the engagement announced at the ball, which makes me suspect he needs to have some promise of future good fortune to keep his creditors at bay."

"There are a number of local entertainments planned for the coming week leading up to the ball. I plan to allow him to get me alone at one of these, and then . . . " Harriet paused for breath, "the three of you will happen to hear my cries of distress, and come find me sobbing hysterically and accusing Matherton of having trying to force himself on me when he found me alone.

That it is a lie won't matter. My bodice will be torn, and with the three of you as unimpeachable witnesses that I was trying to fight him off, he will be disgraced and shunned by Polite Society. Which will make his threats against Kyra harmless. No one will listen to his vitriol anymore."

There was a short silence as the three ladies all looked to Jack and him for a reaction.

This would, decided Rafael, require a very tactful reply. The plan was bold, clever—and far too dangerous to allow. But the concept must be quashed with more than sarcastic laughter to avoid . . .

"It is," announced Jack gravely, "a very well thought-out plan. You have sensed the enemy's weaknesses and exploited them. There are however, some tactical elements which need consideration."

Harriet edged forward in her seat.

"Both Rafe and I have learned through our military experience that one may draw up a perfect strategy, but things rarely go according to plan. For example, how you intend to coordinate Matherton's finding you alone and our being close enough to hear your cries."

"I . . ." Harriet hesitated,

"It is no easy matter to arrange," pointed out Jack. "And there is always the chance that if you stir his interest, he may choose to press his advances on you unexpectedly, assuming you will welcome them. What then?"

"I should fight him off," replied Harriet. "I have been taught some very effective measures for fending off unwanted male attention."

"Have you ever tried them under duress?"

She flushed. "No."

"Theory is all very well," explained Jack. "However, they are not as easy to perform against a bigger, stronger opponent when you are under attack."

After a moment or two, Theo broke the uncomfortable silence with a tentative question. "Have you gentlemen any alternative to Harriet's plan?"

"As a matter of fact, I do," replied Rafael calmly. He looked to Kyra and waited for her to meet his eyes. "I, too, applaud the boldness and bravery of you ladies. But in this instance, I ask that you trust me to handle Matherton. I promise you, by the time the clock chimes midnight on the eve of the ball, he will not be a threat to any of you ladies."

CHAPTER 15

"How . . ." began Harriet, but Kyra quickly cut off any further questions.

"Mr. Greeley is right. Matherton has far too much experience in treachery and conniving. Let us not be guilty of the same hubris he shows—it would be foolhardy to think we can beat him at his own game through our own wiles." She found her voice was surprisingly steady. Somehow the deep sapphirine glow of Rafael's gaze had calmed all her fears.

"So, you are willing to trust Rafe to play the hero?" said Jack with a sly smile.

"Yes. Wholeheartedly," replied Kyra. "Though I do hope you shall lend a hand."

"I doubt he will need me to lift a finger." A twinkle lit in Jack's eye. "But of course, I shall be watching his back."

Harriet looked about to speak up, then seemed to hesitate for a fraction before going on. "You are right, Kyra. It would be foolish not to defer to those who have more practical experience in warfare. And besides, it is your battle to fight, so the final decision must rest with you."

"Absolutely," agreed Theo. "Just tell us how we can help."

Kyra gave her new friends a grateful smile. "Your help has already been invaluable. Indeed, without the support of all of you, I would never have found the strength to stand up to Matherton's threats."

"Love and friendship is a match for any evil," said Rafael softly.

Love. The word sent warmth spiraling through her core. He had not yet said the word in any personal way. Nor had she. But in that instant, it seemed to thrum between them, a mysterious, magical force that defied description.

"Ohhhh." Theo let out a soulful sigh. "What a lovely sentiment. I vow, it makes me feel as if I could slay dragons."

"I'll settled for skewering a dastard," muttered Harriet.

"Which we shall do," replied Rafael.

"I don't suppose you'll tell us what you have in mind?"

"Not at the moment, Miss Farnum. There are several things that need to be put in motion, and if you don't mind, I ought to start without delay. My first visit must be London. When I am sure of the particulars, you ladies will be the first to know."

Both Harriet and Theo rose from the sofa. "Then we should be off."

Jack gave a small stretch and pushed up from his perch on the worktable. "Allow me to escort you home."

"Playing the knight errant?" Harriet's brows rose. "Good heavens, that is not a role you embrace often."

"Actually, I was planning on taking a morning walk for my own health, so have no fear that I am turning altruistic. It is merely killing two birds with one stone."

"Let us hope nothing is slain along the way," replied Harriet dryly. "Especially your reputation for devil-may-care nonchalance."

He appeared amused by her needling and inclined an ironic bow.

Though loath to leave Rafael's comforting presence, Kyra gathered her skirts and rose as well.

"A moment, Lady Kyra," he said. "Might I have a private word with you before you go?"

Jack's lazy grin turned more serious. "Shall we wait? I doubt Matherton is still lurking in the woods, but for now it is probably best to err on the side of caution."

"No need," replied Rafael. "I shall see Lady Kyra home."

His cousin snapped off a jaunty salute and the door closed, leaving the two of them alone.

For a moment neither of them moved.

"Matherton didn't touch you, did he?" Though his voice was barely above a whisper, it had a steely edge that steadied her nerves. "He didn't hurt you?"

"No, he merely unsettled me with his sudden appearance."

He said something low and rough in Spanish, and as the light gilded his profile, a finespun gold ridging the olive-dark chiseling of his features, she was reminded that there was a harder side—a warrior side—to him.

A flicker of a smile suddenly softened his face. "Ah, *querida.* Just a little while longer and then you need never fear him again."

Hard yet soft. Strong, yet sensitive. And an infinite range of intriguing nuances that would need a lifetime to explore.

"Strangely enough, I fear nothing when you are near," she whispered. "Not even my own doubts and weaknesses."

"Then I hope . . ." Two swift steps and suddenly she was enfolded in his arms. "I hope you will allow me to always be close."

Kyra pressed her cheek to his shoulder, reveling in the warmth of his skin pulsing through the layers of wool and linen, the spicy scent of shaving soap, the reassuring strength of his hold. "Would that it were possible."

He gently tucked the wind-loosened strands of hair behind

her ear. "It is, *querida*. You have only to say 'yes" to my proposal of marriage."

"You can't want to marry me," she rasped, once she had swallowed the lump in her throat.

Rafael lifted her face, and through her tear-pearled lashes, all she could see was the jewel-bright glitter of his sapphire eyes. "But I do."

"I'm reckless, I'm selfish, I'm tainted with scandal, I'm . . ." She sucked in a ragged breath. "I'm all wrong for you."

"You're passionate, you're kind-hearted, you're imaginative, you're full of life." Rafael brushed a kiss to her brow. "You're perfect for me."

"But—"

He touched a fingertip to her lips. "Come, my love, let us look to the future, not the past."

Love. Rafael loved her?

Her heart skipped a beat, and then suddenly that fleeting whisper of breath gave her the courage to believe that old mistakes might be left behind.

"Truly? You wish to marry me?"

The curl of his mouth sent a wave of joy undulating through her body. "If you'll have me."

Wrapping her arms around him, she hugged him close. "I want you truly, madly, fiercely." Tears were coursing down her cheeks. "I love you so much it hurts."

A kiss blotted the salt from her skin. Then his mouth found hers and all she tasted was a sweetness beyond words.

"It is time to leave pain behind you," he said quietly after a lengthy embrace. "Together, let us feel only happiness and excitement for all the wonder that we shall share."

"Yes," said Kyra. "Yes, yes, yes."

"Dare I hope that one of those means you've consented to be my wife?"

"Yes." She smiled and then said it again.

"*Bueno.*" Rafael leaned in, his breath tickling her lips. "Then I may, in good conscience, give you a *real* kiss.

❧

AT HER SHUDDERING RESPONSE, a clench of desire took hold of him. That she took pleasure in his touch filled him with elation—they were entwined, body and spirit in perfect harmony.

Dios Madre, it took all of his self-control to remember that he must behave as a perfect gentleman. She had been betrayed by a dastard unworthy of the title, and not for the world would he have her think that he would trifle with her honor.

Rafael let his mouth linger a moment longer, drinking in the ethereal taste of her essence—a delicate spice far more nuanced than the finest chocolate. Then he reluctantly pulled back a fraction.

The loss of her warmth suddenly made his skin feel chilled despite the motes of sunlight dancing all around them.

She, too, seemed to feel bereft of the connection. A wordless protest sounded in her throat as her eyes slowly opened. Their color—a smoky, sensuous hue that nearly made him come undone—flickered through her lashes.

"Must we stop?" she asked.

"I fear so, else I shall give way to primal urges."

"I don't mind."

"Ah, don't tempt me, *querida*." Rafael kissed the tip of her nose. "We shall have a lifetime to explore our passions after the wedding. But until then, I will distract myself from your glorious charms by concentrating on how to see that Matherton is well punished for his sins.

The mention of her tormentor drove some of the color from Kyra's cheeks. "Please don't do anything dangerous," she said, her voice turning taut with tension. "I couldn't bear it if you were hurt."

"I won't be," he assured her. "What I have in mind will be far more effective than a physical pummeling."

"What—"

"Nay, my love. You'll learn of the details once I have everything arranged. Until then, just trust me."

The look of alarm gave way to a smile. "With all my heart."

It was all he could do to keep from enfolding her in another long and lingering embrace. "Come, let me see you home, and then I must be off to London."

"W-will you be gone long?" she asked as they cut across the back lawns and turned down the footpath connecting the two estates.

"A night, maybe two," answered Rafael. He took several strides before adding, "I've a difficult task to ask of you, but it plays a key role in bringing about Matherton's ultimate demise."

"Whatever it is, I shall gladly do it."

"You mentioned that he plans on paying a call on you and your father."

She nodded. "Yes, he will press me to agree to announce the betrothal. I imagine he thinks doing so at the manor will remind me that the threat he is making can ruin all that Papa holds dear."

"I want you to agree."

A spasm of surprise crossed her face, but she quickly composed herself. "I . . .very well. But what shall I tell Papa? I don't think he will believe my heart is engaged." A sigh. "And I'd rather not tell him any lies. He's been hurt enough by this whole sordid affair."

He thought for a moment. "Why not tell him the truth?

Kyra turned so abruptly that her half boot snagged on a root and caused her to stumble. "You mean all about Matherton's threat? But then he would know the truth about everything."

"Love, friendship, trust," he said. "You've seen what powerful forces they are when you dare to believe in them."

In the long, leafy shadows, her expression flickered between wary and thoughtful.

"It is, of course, your decision what details you choose to share with your father," he went on. "But if you prefer to simply ask that he spread the word to the guests that a betrothal will be announced at midnight, it would not be a lie. And in fact, it would make Matherton confident that all is going as he planned."

"But you think I should tell him everything?"

He shook his head. "Nay, I shall never presume to tell you what you ought to do, Kyra. I respect your judgment. Only you can decide what is best."

"You are," she said, "a most remarkable man in every way."

"I hope you won't be disappointed when you discover my many foibles," he said wryly.

Kyra reached for his hand and lifted it to her lips. "You could never disappoint me," she said, brushing a kiss to the back of his knuckles.

They walked on in companionable silence, skirting the apple orchard and making their way up the sloping lawns to the back terrace.

"If you wish for me to come in and speak with your Father, I would be happy to do so," he said.

"You are fighting enough of my battles for me. This is one that I must handle myself."

"Trust—you must trust yourself. Just remember, whatever you choose to tell your father, our real plans must remain a secret. Matherton mustn't guess that he will be dancing to a very unpleasant tune at Jack's ball." A glance showed that none of the gardeners were working close by, so he caught her in a quick embrace. "I must be off, then. Until later."

"Please promise me to be careful, Rafael," she said abruptly as he turned to retrace his steps.

He gave her a reassuring smile. "Don't worry, *querida*. I am always a very cautious fellow. War quickly teaches you never to underestimate an enemy."

"It's just that I've come to see that Matherton is diabolically cunning and has no scruples. That makes him dangerous."

"So am I," he replied quietly. "Far more than he is when those I love are threatened."

The shadows clouding her gaze lightened.

"You need not be fearful on my account," he went on. "And as for you, I wouldn't leave you if I thought there was any chance of trouble."

Though a touch of trepidation lingered, she forced a small laugh. "I feel quite safe with Hero and Harriet guarding against any mischief."

"A formidable pair, indeed." Rafael pressed his fingers to his lips and blew her a kiss. "*Adios, querida.* Unless I am much mistaken, when I return, I shall have the means to make Matherton quickly learn he has made a grave mistake in thinking you are alone and at the mercy of his machinations."

KYRA PAUSED in front of the foyer mirror to remove her bonnet and re-pin the errant wisps of windblown hair. How strange, she mused, touching her fingertips to where Rafael's kiss still tingled on her lips. Her face appeared unchanged a whit since her morning ablutions, and yet she felt like an entirely different person.

Like a phoenix, rising in multi-colored splendor from a pile of ash-gray coals. A fanciful, fairytale image, perhaps. But she was in a fanciful, fairy tale sort of mood, where happily-ever-after stories seemed possible.

A magical bird could be reborn with glorious new plumage. A sleeping princess could be awoken from a dark, deathlike sleep by a prince's kiss.

Her dreamy sigh fogged the glass, drawing her back from such thoughts. She quickly straightened her bodice and smoothed her skirts, then turned resolutely and headed for the stairs.

The duke was at work in his study. A gruff growl answered her knock, but undeterred, she pushed the door open.

"Forgive me for disturbing you Papa, but might I have a word with you?"

"Oh, it's you, my dear, of course, of course." Grimacing, he took off his spectacles and dropped them on the blotter. "I thought it was Mifflin, come to badger me about planting mangel-wurzels instead of turnips in the south fields."

"You are opposed to the idea?"

"All these havey-cavey ideas about agriculture," grumbled the duke. "I would much rather have my nose buried in a history book than a boring treatise on soil nutrients and crop rotation."

"You are very fond of Mifflin," she reminded him. "And all his other suggestions have turned out very well."

He blew out his cheeks. "So they have." A grin tugged at his mouth. "I will eventually allow myself to be dragged into the new century, but I shall go kicking and screaming."

"I cannot quite picture you kicking and screaming, Papa. You are far too distinguished. And besides, your valet would swoon if you were to scuff the mirror-like gloss of your Hessians. Gorman confided to me that, like Brummel, he uses champagne in his special polish."

Her father chuckled. "Does he? I shall have to add a new lock to the wine cellar." The laughter then slowly faded from his face. "Do I appear such a pompous popinjay to you?" he asked hesitantly. "I know it was very hard on you girls, losing your mother at such an early age. I have tried, but ..."

Kyra crossed the carpet and placed a hand on his shoulder. "You have been a wonderful parent, Papa. It is I who have ..." She drew in a deep breath. "But perhaps we should both stop looking to the past and focus on the future."

He covered her hand with his.

"As to that, I wish to discuss a matter concerning the upcoming ball."

"If there is a problem with the hothouses and the flowers—"

"No, no, the flowers are looking splendid. It has to do with . . ."

How to broach the subject? Despite Rafael's encouragement, it still was not easy to speak about her folly, especially to her father.

But as the silence grew louder, Rafael's words began to echo softly inside her head. *Trustlovetrustlove.*

Trust. Love. Trust love.

"It has to do with Lord Matherton."

The duke's eyes clouded with concern.

Dropping her gaze, she went, "He is visiting the area and will be attending the ball as part of Lord Dunster's party. I encountered him several days ago during one of my walks, and we have spoken several times since then."

"I see." Her father's voice was expressionless.

"He will likely be calling here," said Kyra. "To pay his respects."

Her gaze was fixed on the far windows, but even so, she was acutely aware of his searching stare. "With your blessing?"

She hesitated in answering.

"I had not thought your affections were still engaged, not after the way he abandoned you after the accident." The tightly measured control of his voice then betrayed a ripple of emotion as he muttered, "It was a damned ungentlemanly and cowardly thing to do."

"I thought you approved of him."

The duke rubbed at his brow. "You seemed to have had your heart set on him, and as your mother and I had made a love match against my own father's wishes, I did not wish to play the tyrant with you. Matherton was from a good family, and I knew nothing to his discredit, save for the fact that his charm seemed too oily for my taste. In retrospect—"

"In retrospect, I should have seen him for what he was," she blurted out. "A schemer who cared more for my dowry and your patronage than he ever did for me."

Levering his broad bulk out of his chair, he enfolded her in a fatherly hug. The faint crackle of starch and scent of his shaving soap brought a rush of childhood memories. How dearly she had missed the safe haven of his arms.

"Oh, Papa," she mumbled against his shoulder. "What a fool I have been."

"Let us have none of that, missy" said the duke gruffly. "If anyone has been the fool, it is I. But that is all behind us."

Kyra held him tightly, savoring the comforting warmth of his body and steady pulsing of his heart. *Touch and feel*—Rafael had made her so joyfully aware that physical connection was a powerful part of love.

"As for Matherton, have no fear that he will pester you anymore. When that jackanape shows up at the door, I shall send him away with a flea in his ear."

"No!" she exclaimed, pulling back in alarm. "That is, it's not quite so simple."

Her father's brow furrowed in question.

"I . . ." Her newfound courage faltered. "I would rather not explain all the details, Papa." There were some things a father shouldn't have to know. "He has made some threats."

"The scoundrel!" rasped the duke. "I shall darken his deadlights—"

"I have every confidence that he will be punished for his perfidy, Papa. But please, you mustn't go off half-cocked. You see, Mr. Greeley has a plan."

"Greeley, eh?" His look of rage gave way to a more bemused expression. "Now there is a steady, sensible fellow." He picked up his spectacles and polished them on his sleeve, then set them down again. "I like him."

Kyra felt a flush steal to her cheeks. "Yes, so do I."

The duke cleared his throat with a small cough. "He has a plan, you say?"

"Actually, I am not quite sure what he has in mind. He left for London this morning in order to search out information. Don't ask me what, for he didn't say. He simply asked me to trust him, and, well, I am happy to do so." Feeling a little awkward, she quickly added, "After all, he is Jack's cousin. And Jack is involved as well."

"Ah, well, then I suppose I can rest easy that the matter is in capable hands," her father said. "Those two young war heroes should have no trouble defeating a lily-livered coward."

She hoped that was true. But a frisson of worry slid down her spine. Matherton didn't play by gentlemanly rules, while Rafael and Jack were the very souls of honor.

"Yes, if all goes according to plan. But we all have a part to play in it, Papa."

"Excellent. I do hope it calls for me to have my Manton pistols loaded and primed," quipped her father. He flexed a fist. "Though in truth I would rather plant that scoundrel a facer."

"I trust it won't come to firearms or fisticuffs," answered Kyra. "Rafael—that, is, Mr. Greeley, would simply like for you to make it known that in addition to celebrating Jack's return, a special betrothal announcement will be made at the ball."

The duke sat up a little straighter in his chair. "A *betrothal?*"

Kyra was sure her face was now flame red. "Yes, Matherton is pressing me to agree to marry him, and in order to keep him off guard, I must pretend to accede to the demand. Having the guests all abuzz about the surprise announcement will further lull him into a false sense of security."

"Mr. Greeley is to be commended for having devised such a clever ruse."

"Yes, well, he and Jack have a great deal of experience in planning tactics and strategies to defeat a cunning enemy."

"Thank heavens for that." Her father pursed his lips. "The guests will of course be disappointed that it is all a hoax. Tell me, did Greeley give any hint as to how I should deal with that?"

"I . . ." *Was that a twinkle lurking in the depths of her father's eye?* "Perhaps it would be best if you speak to him about that, Papa. I wouldn't want to garble any of the details."

"Yes, perhaps that would be best." It was definitely a twinkle. "Indeed, I am very much looking forward to what the clever lad has to say."

CHAPTER 16

"That was exceedingly clever of you, sir," said Harriet admiringly as she set down her cup.

"Thank you," replied Rafael. He had just finished showing them the documents he had brought back from London and explaining how all the pieces of his plan now fit together.

"Though I still would have liked to see Matherton unmasked for the vile seducer he is," she said.

"Sweet is revenge, especially to women," Jack said. "Or so says Lord Byron, upon whom all you ladies seem to dote."

"Lord Byron is a very astute observer of human nature," replied Harriet.

"And a man very familiar with vice."

Theo sighed. "Yes, but any man who pens a poem like 'She walks in Beauty Like the Night' can be forgiven a multitude of sins."

"Matherton will pay for his sins," pointed out Rafael, before the conversation could veer off from the subject at hand. He, too, loved literature but for now they had real life drama to deal with. "Perhaps not with public shame, but what matters is he'll no longer be a predator in gentleman's clothes, free to prey on an unsuspecting young lady."

"I confess, I am curious as to how you managed to uncover the proof of Matherton's gambling debts and the affidavit from Berkeley concerning the cheating at cards," said Jack. "You had only a day in Town, and while I know your skill at ferreting out vital information during wartime, what you faced was no easy task." A grin. "Don't tell me love has given you supernatural powers."

Rafael and Kyra had shared the news of their engagement with their friends, with the strict admonition that it must remain a secret until the evening of the ball.

"Don't needle them," chided Harriet. "*You* may have no poetry in your soul, but love is not a sentiment to be mocked."

"I was teasing, not mocking. There is a difference," said Jack. "And by the by, since when have you become a staunch defender of fluttery hearts and flowery poems? You are usually far more sarcastic than I am about *amour*."

Harriet colored, but before she could answer Kyra quickly intervened. "You may tease me and Rafael to your heart's content, Jack. I expect no less. But at the moment, we have more serious things to discuss."

"As to your question," interjected Rafael, "My trip involved no magic incantations, merely a trip to Horse Guards. Anthony Harding, our old comrade, is in charge of coordinating military intelligence both at home and abroad. The position gives him access to a great many networks of information. And as he owed me a favor or two, he was willing to help, especially when he heard that Matherton is a thoroughly dirty dish."

Theo shifted on the sofa. "That was excellent thinking, sir. So rather than us having to create any dramatic scene, you mean to simply take Matherton aside at some point during the festivities, show him the proofs you have of his perfidy, and suggest that he better decamp for the Continent if he wishes to avoid having you call in his vowels."

"That was perhaps the cleverest thing of all, to have purchased all his debts from his creditors," mused Jack. "You can ruin him in the blink of an eye."

"It must have cost you a fortune," said Kyra.

"Peace of mind can't be measured in pounds and pence. And I assure you, I could well afford the price."

"Then we'll speak no more of it," said Jack decisively. "What we do need to discuss is strategy for the next few days. Matherton will be attending the supper party given by Lady Theo's aunt and uncle tonight. What do you wish for our two stalwart lady co-conspirators to do?"

"Nothing so dangerous as to offer yourself as bait," replied Rafael as he locked eyes with Harriet. "Simply make a point of gossiping about a mystery engagement that will be announced at the ball. Coy hints about it likely being the duke's daughter will stir speculation, and serve to make Matherton confident that all is going according to his plans."

"*Over*confident, we hope," added Theo.

He nodded.

"That seems simple enough." Harriet sounded a trifle disappointed, but to her credit she didn't complain. "And the night of the ball?"

"There should," he answered with a faint smile, "be even less call for action, other than dancing. I suggest you simply enjoy the festivities."

"I wish . . ." began Kyra before faltering into silence again.

"Wish what?" inquired Harriet.

Her mouth tugging into a rueful grimace, Kyra shook her head. "Never mind, it was a silly thought."

"Nonetheless, I should like to hear it," pressed Rafael. "In battle, we soldiers learn to pay attention to our instincts."

"Now I feel even more foolish," she said. "It's nothing I can articulate—it's just a wish that this were all over."

"It soon will be, *querida*."

The endearment slipped out of its own accord. Harriet and Theo both ducked their heads to hide a grin, but Jack, as was his wont, was less tactful.

"Wishing for the end," he quipped. "And yearning for the beginning." A theatrical sigh punctuated his words. "Of married life, that is, and all the delights it offers."

Kyra turned beet red.

"Just because *you* have no poetry in your soul doesn't mean you have to put Kyra to blush for feeling so happy."

"She knows me well enough to understand my peculiar sense of humor."

"That does not mean she appreciates it."

Jack opened his mouth to retort, and then shut it. "You see," he said through clenched teeth. "I am capable of exercising discretion when I put my mind to it."

Theo smothered a laugh.

"Though clearly it is a sore trial," said Kyra. "Do stop that grinding. Your molars sound in danger of cracking."

"*Et tu*, Brutus?"

Harriet exaggerated a gasp of surprise. "Good Heavens, he might not appreciate Byron's poetry, but at least he had read some of the Bard's plays."

Seeing the tension melt from Kyra's face as she joined in the banter, Rafael decided that Jack deserved more credit for astute observation than he usually received. His outrageous teasing had distracted her from her worries about Matherton and helped her relax. Whether Harriet understood what he was doing, playing the foil to his rapier was another question.

But at present, it was not one he was at liberty to mull over.

"Perhaps he has only seen it on the stage," suggested Kyra. "I am not entirely convinced that Jack knows how to read. There were an awful lot of 'No Trespassing' signs blatantly ignored when we were out gallivanting across the countryside."

Heaving a gusty sigh, Jack rose. "On that note, perhaps I should take my leave, before my character is further savaged."

"Oh, look—he knows how to make a dramatic exit, too," Harriet said.

He tried to look offended, but amusement danced in his eyes.

"Let us hope we have no drama in the next few days save for this playacting," said Theo.

~

"ARE YOU NERVOUS?"

Rafael smoothed the last folds of his cravat into place before turning around from the cheval glass. "Should I be?"

The evening of the ball had finally arrived, and rather than trepidation, he felt only a sense of calm purpose.

"One always feels a flutter of butterflies in one's belly just before battle," replied Jack with a grin. "You're not only crossing swords with a villain but also announcing your betrothal, assuming the duke gives you his blessing instead of tossing you into the frog pond. That might make even St. George a little knock-kneed. After all, he merely had to slay a dragon."

"I may not be a saint," quipped Rafael. "But trust me, Evil doesn't stand a chance tonight. Besides, I am confident that Matherton will have no weapon to counter the documents I now possess, so rather than a battle, I expect him to flee without a fight. As for the duke . . ." He brushed a shock of hair back from his brow. "If I can't convince him that I love his daughter, then I don't deserve her."

"His Grace can be a very intimidating fellow," his cousin said. "My ears are still scorched from several of the set-downs he gave me."

"I don't intend to pilfer a dozen bottles of his most costly champagne from the wine cellar, so the meeting won't begin with him belching fire and brimstone."

"But you *are* planning to ride off into the golden glow of the sunset with his daughter."

"You have been reading too many of Mrs. Radcliffe's horrid novels," countered Rafael. "That happened in *The Italian*. In case you have forgotten, I am Spanish, and thus will do things a little differently."

"Half Spanish," corrected Jack. "Your hot Latin blood is tempered with the ice of Nordic Vikings. Which probably accounts for why you are so cool in the heat of battle." A pause. "I still say you may need that *sang froid* when you face His Grace."

"I don't plan to melt under his gaze."

"Aye, I suppose we've faced too many baptisms by fire to fear the ire of a father, even if he is a duke." Jack shifted slightly "One last thing—are you planning to confront Matherton unarmed?"

"A weapon would ruin the cut of my evening coat." Eying the bulge in his cousin's coat pocket, he grinned. "Speaking of which, you need to make a few last-minute sartorial adjustments. As the guest of honor, you ought not appear looking like an itinerate peddler."

"My attire shall look faultless." Jack withdrew a small turn-off pocket pistol from its hiding place. "As for you, I suggest that fashion give way to prudence."

"I don't need that," he said flatly.

"Nonetheless, you'll take it. Matherton is a poisonous snake, and has fangs. Don't underestimate how dangerous such a reptile can be."

Though tempted to refuse, Rafael relented and accepted the weapon. Slipping it inside his waistband, he tugged the front of his coat back into place. "There. Now that I have humored you, are we ready to be off?"

"But of course." It wouldn't do to be late to the party."

❧

"HOW NICE TO SEE THE Manor alive with lights and colors," said the duke. He paused at the entrance to the ballroom, his gaze sweeping over the glittering chandeliers and profusion of pastel blooms before he turned to smile at Kyra. "The flower arrangements look magnificent, my dear. Indeed, everything looks perfect. This will be an evening to remember."

"Jack deserves no less," she said softly.

"True," he replied, a twinkle of candlelight reflecting from the diamond-paned windows to add a touch of sparkle to his eyes. "But I think he would agree that what we are really celebrating is family and friends."

And the love that ties us all together, thought Kyra. Heeding Rafael's words of caution that they must be mindful of doing nothing to put Matherton on guard, she decided not to say it aloud. But when the clock chimed midnight . . .

Stealing a glance at her father's profile, she had a feeling he needed no words to sense the happiness bubbling up inside her.

The duke gave the room one more appraising look, then cleared his throat with a brusque cough. "I wish your mother could see how lovely you look tonight. And Lexy. They would both be so proud of you."

Kyra blinked back tears, but managed a smile. "I shall try to be worthy of their memory, Papa."

"You already are. And more, my dear." He took a small oblong box from his pocket and opened it. "This was your mother's."

Nestled on a bed of midnight blue velvet was a simple strand of perfectly matched pearls with a teardrop emerald pendant.

"I had planned on giving it to you on your betrothal, but, well, I confess that something held me back."

"Why now?" she asked.

"Oh, let us just say that it feels like the right moment." The duke undid the gold clasp and carefully fastened it around her neck. "It suits you very well." His voice turned husky with emotion. "You look like a fairy princess."

"I'm even luckier. I'm a duke's daughter."

Her father gave her a quick hug before stepping back with a gruff chuckle. "Heaven forbid that I crumple that ethereal ball-gown, so I shall refrain from a more crushing embrace. The silk and ruffles look like they are made out of spun sugar."

Her clothing might be delicate, but Kyra no longer felt fragile.

"Now, I had better get Gorman and make one last check that all is in order in the wine cellar. The guests will be arriving soon."

The duke set off down the corridor, and Kyra was about to follow when a flutter of the draperies at the far end of the ball-room caught her eye. The heavy gold-threaded damask fabric moved again in the breeze, revealing a scattering of pale pink petals on the dark dance floor.

Hurrying across the polished parquet, she found that one of the vases on the decorative plinth had tipped over, spilling the carefully arranged flowers. The latch must have come loose in the breeze, she decided, allowing the brass casement to swing open.

"Damnation." The damage could be covered up by rear-ranging the other vases, and no one would be the wiser. But the symmetry would be ruined, and she wanted everything to be just right.

Kyra hesitated. The hothouses were only a short distance away. If she went out through the music room and cut across the back terrace, it would take no more than ten minutes to replace the bouquet. She stared down at the pristine hem of her gown. It would likely not survive the trip outdoors unscathed.

"What does it matter if a bit of grass and mud clings to my skirts," she said. "After all, I'm a slightly soiled dove, so it's an apt metaphor." In the past, the thought would have greatly upset her, but now it only provoked a rueful smile. Let the gossips titter over lurid speculations if they wished. She wanted every last detail to be perfect for Jack.

And for Rafael.

Hitching up her gown, she hurried through the side salon and made her way out to the graveled walkway leading past the conservatory. The nightingales had struck up their evening serenade, and the soft song wafted through the swaying branches of the high privet hedge. As she rounded the bend leading off to the hothouses, a dark shape burst out from the glade copper beeches, startling her into a stumble.

"Woof."

"Oh fie, you naughty hound," Kyra scolded, once she had steadied her nerves. "How did you slip away from Anna?" Her maid had promised to keep Hero—and his overexuberant paws—away from the festivities, but clearly he had other ideas.

He wagged his tail and with a canine grin appeared to be eyeing the tails of her satin sash.

"This is no time for rough-and-tumble games. One snap of your teeth, one swipe of those muddy paws and you'll be on a diet of bread and water for the next month!"

Hero pricked up his ears and obediently fell in step beside her, close but not too close.

"I see you are a *very* intelligent dog," she added with a light laugh. "You've learned your lessons well."

"Unlike his mistress." Matherton darted out from the trees and grabbed rough hold of her arm. "I guessed that you would be stupid enough to come fetch new flowers to replace the ones I knocked over."

She tried to pull free, but his hand tighten like a vise around her flesh. "And call off your cur." He brandished a spiked cudgel as Hero bared his teeth and gave a menacing growl. "Or I'll bash the beast's skull."

"No, Hero!" she rasped. "Back! Back!"

The hound retreated, just out of arm's reach.

"What madness is this, sir—she began, but her former fiancé silenced her with a hard shake.

"Stubble the chatter," he snapped. "I warned you that there would be consequences if you defied me."

"I haven't—"

"Liar!" He rapped his cudgel against the vase in her hands, shattering the delicate porcelain. "I've learned that Spanish half breed has been sniffing around London, asking questions about my affairs."

Kyra decided protests were futile. Lifting her chin, she answered, "And he's learned enough sordid details to put an end to your foul machinations. So unhand me and leave Pierpont Manor."

"Oh, I will be leaving the Manor, seeing as your mongrel lapdog has forced me to change plans." Swift as a serpent, Matherton twisted her arm behind her back, and pressed the point of the cudgel against her throat. "But you are coming with me."

Fear spiked through her as the cold steel bit into her flesh. But thoughts of Rafael and a future together gave her courage—she struggled to break away.

Snarling an oath, Matherton shifted his hold, jamming the cudgel hard against her ribs while slapping his other hand over her mouth.

Kyra fought, but he was too strong, and the breath was being squeezed from her lungs. When he lifted her off her feet and swung around for the trees, she was powerless to resist.

"There will be a wedding as soon as we reach Gretna Green, and then I will most definitely be returning to Pierpont Manor to collect the dowry and patronage that your father will have no choice but to give me."

Dear God, the man was truly a monster.

As for you . . ." Another rough shake. "You will soon learn never again to defy my wishes."

Hero lunged and managed to seize her sash. A lashing kick from her abductor smashed against his jaws, but he held fast.

"Plaguey cur," grunted Matherton as he jerked her around and kicked out again. Loosened by all the tugging, the smooth satin slipped out of its bow and slithered to the ground.

He whirled again and set off with a loping stride along the narrow footpath. A wave of nausea washed over her as the jagged shadows spun wildly before her eyes. But she willed herself not to swoon. While there was still a breath left in her body, she would not give in to despair.

Scotland was a long way from Kent, and surely the power of Love was more than a match for the power of Evil.

CHAPTER 17

"You ladies will be the belles of the ball," Jack said as he and Rafael helped Harriet and Theo into the earl's carriage.

"Indeed," chimed in Hendrie. "You must promise me the pleasure of a dance, that is, if these two jackanapes haven't already seized all the spots on your dance card."

"You are kind, sirs. Too kind, in fact." Harriet settled herself on the plush seat and smoothed out the skirts of her gown. "I am quite aware that my looks are no more than ordinary, but as tonight has a certain fairy tale magic to it, I shall pretend your flummeries are real."

"I never flumm," drawled Jack.

Theo laughed as she tugged at her elegant kidskin gloves. Rafael noted that her eyes were sparkling with excitement in the glow of the oil lamp.

"Nor do I," he added. "And the so-called glittering Diamonds of the First Water will look dull and lifeless compared to the grace and spirit that shines from the pair of you."

Both ladies blinked, and for once, Harriet appeared speechless.

It was Theo who recovered her voice first. "Flumm or not, I am exceedingly grateful to you gentlemen for making me feel like a princess tonight." A fluttery sigh slipped from her lips. "Dancing, champagne—I shall savor every moment until midnight, when I turn back into a plump toad." She made a rueful face. "Or is it a pumpkin?"

"Perhaps," Rafael said, "you will make your own magic, a spell that will long outlast any fairy dust."

Her expression turned pensive.

"Mrs. Ganton went to the Manor this afternoon to help with some of the last minute arrangements," said Hendrie, craning his neck to peer out the carriage window at the vehicle passed through one of the side entrances to the estate. "She says the flower arrangements are magnificent and that the myriad candles will blaze brighter than the solstice sun. I wonder . . ." His voice trailed off.

Jack leaned forward in his seat. "What is it, Father?"

"I'm not sure," confessed Hendrie. "There looks to be an animal running along the road, dragging . . . I can't quite make it out, save for that it seems to be a long, light-colored piece of fabric."

Mystified, Harriet and Theo peered through glass panes by their seat.

"Why, it looks like a sash," announced Theo after a moment.

"Good Lord, it's Hero," exclaimed Harriet. "And the sash is just like the one gracing the gown Kyra planned to wear tonight. She showed it to us yesterday."

Rafael was already rapping on the trap to order the coachman to halt the horses. Before the wheels rolled to a halt, he wrenched open the door and jumped down to the road.

On seeing him, the exhausted hound mustered a last sprint and dropped the sash by his feet.

Woof, woof. Hero whined and tugged at his sleeve as he

reached to pick up the muddy length of satin. The smoothness of the fabric sent a cold shiver galloping down his spine.

Jack dropped down beside him. "Damnation," he muttered under his breath so the others wouldn't hear. "Something's gone terribly wrong."

"I should have been more alert," said Rafael tightly. He had made the mistake of underestimating Matherton's cunning.

Hero tugged at his coat again, and backed away, pulling him off-balance.

"Yes, yes, *amigo*. Take me to her."

"I'm coming with you," said Jack.

"No!" He pushed his cousin back toward the carriage. "Take the others to the ball. You're the guest of honor and your absence will stir questions. There may be a way to avoid scandal if we act quickly."

Harriet poked her head out the open door. "What can we do to help?"

"Think of some excuse on why Kyra is not greeting the guests. A headache, a twisted ankle—bloody hell, the plague! Anything!"

"Leave it to us," came the grim reply. "Now *go!*

Hero was dancing impatiently, his growls growing louder. Seeing Rafael rise, the hound whirled and raced off toward the glade of beech trees bordering the drive.

"Move faster, damn you." Matherton punctuated his order with a rough shove. He had put her down once they were hidden in the tangle of the trees and was now half dragging her along the narrow footpath. She guessed he must have a carriage waiting somewhere on one of the cart roads crisscrossing the estate.

"Ballroom slippers are not made for woodland treks," she replied, stumbling yet again as her gown snagged on a twist of brambles. "Nor," she added defiantly, "do I dance to your tune."

He swore again and yanked the fabric free. "You won't dare step out of line once I've made you my bride." A nasty laugh rumbled through the overhanging leaves. "Remember, a wife's duty is to honor and obey."

I will never be your wife, Kyra vowed. Drawing a deep breath, she made herself gather her wits. It was imperative to stay alert. She knew the estate like the back of her hand, and if she could choose the right place to break free, there was a chance she could evade recapture.

If only she wasn't hampered by her cursed skirts! But Matherton looked even more uncomfortable in the woods. Slapping at the branches, stumbling over the roots, he was swearing most foully. In a footrace over rough ground, she just might win.

Looking around, Kyra saw they were heading in the direction of the river and the stone bridge leading to the abbey ruins. *The abbey ruins.* Squeezing her eyes shut, she forced herself not to think of that fateful evening. That was in the past—having Rafael in her life gave her the courage to believe tonight would not bring another tragedy. With that in mind, every few steps she made a point of snapping a twig or stamping a footprint in the damp earth. Not that she had any real hope of Rafael discovering what had happened, but the small actions helped to buck up her spirits.

After thrashing to the top of a steep rise in the way, Matherton halted to wipe the sweat from his brow. His carefully cultivated aura of polished charm had given way to edgy agitation. He looked desperate. Which of course made him more dangerous than ever.

"Bloody Hell, how much farther to the bridge?" he asked.

"Maybe a half mile," she replied, deliberately exaggerating the distance.

He swore again and raked a hand through his disheveled curls as his gaze lingered uncertainly on the fork up ahead. "Which way? And I warn you, don't trifle with me or you'll be very sorry for it."

"To the right," answered Kyra without hesitation. Both ways led to the river path, but the left was far shorter. "Be assured, milord, I realize that I am at your mercy."

Her meek reply seemed to steady his jumpy nerves. Though he kept a grip on her arm as he started forward, it relaxed ever so slightly. Bidding her time, she moved with him. When the right moment came, she would be ready to seize it.

And if the right moment didn't come? Well, she would simply have to make her own luck.

HACKLES RAISED, Hero circled the shattered vase that lay in the middle of the garden walkway, emitting a mix of whines and growls. Rafael studied the scuffs in the gravel, needing only a moment to read what had happened. A struggle, and it took little imagination to picture the confrontation. Matherton had stolen a march on him. However, the dastard couldn't have much of a headstart, and logistics dictated that his carriage was hidden some distance away to avoid being spotted by any of the revelers. Familiar with the area through his daily walks, Rafael quickly decided there were only two likely possibilities. But he couldn't afford to make a mistake

"Kyra—find Kyra!" he said to Hero.

The hound had already anticipated the order. Tail waving like a battle flag, he raced to the footpath leading through the sloping grove of trees to the left of the hothouses and turned with a low bark.

Rafael was after him like a pistol shot. "We must move quickly, *amigo*. Once he gets her to a carriage, our chances of stopping his nefarious plans become far more difficult."

He could well guess what Matherton had in mind. Marriage

was the miscreant's only hope of dodging ruin, so he would be heading to the Scottish border to force an over-the-anvil union. That Kyra would refuse would not matter. There were far too many unscrupulous men willing to overlook a drugged or bruised lady and perform the simple rites for a price. The legalities could be contested, but the damage would be done. It could take ages to unknot the tangle of conflicting claims, giving Matherton a powerful hold over the duke.

As for Kyra, she would not be free.

No, he must catch them now, before they took to the roads and the trail grew too cold. And when he did . . .

He took no pleasure in violence, but at the moment he would have cut out Matherton's liver without batting an eye.

Nose to the ground, Hero zigzagged back and forth through the underbrush but kept following the footpath. Twilight was deepening, making it difficult to see. But as he round a thicket of brambles, Rafael caught sight of a few gossamer threads of pale silk hanging from the thorns.

"*Bueno*," he said under his breath. A moment later, the sound was echoed by the hound's low *woof*, as he hesitated at a fork in the path, and then swung to the right.

A broken twig, a deep footprint—Kyra was leaving a clear trail to follow now. A fleeting smile tugged at his mouth. She was pluck to the bone, even when she must be frightened and acutely aware that the odds of being rescued were not in her favor.

Rafael quickened his pace, intent on changing those odds. Matherton may have won the first skirmish, but the battle was far from over.

Up ahead, he saw Hero slow to a stiff-legged walk, his ears flattening, his hackles rising. A low growl reverberated in his throat. Rafael hurried to his side and crouched down. "Silence, *amigo*."

The sounds ceased.

Rafael cocked his head to listen. Over the faint swirl of

eddying river, he heard the slipping and sliding of footsteps. Taking a firm hold of the hound's collar, he started forward, a swift, silent predator, stalking his prey. Picking his way over the rough ground, he kept to the higher ground, and at the next small bend, he spotted Matherton and Kyra walking along the narrow path at the river's edge.

Slowly, slowly, he crept closer—close enough to overhear what was being said.

With his hair in disarray and his bedraggled evening clothes spattered with mud, Matherton looked like a demon just dragged up from some underworld cesspool. His mood was apparently equally foul, for he was in the midst of needling Kyra about her fateful accident..

"Ah, this stretch of riverbank brings back memories, does it not? If you hadn't been so reckless, I'd be well-settled in an advantageous marriage, and enjoying all the special favors that go along with being the son-in-law of a duke." A pause. "You caused me a great deal of trouble."

When Kyra didn't answer him, he added, "And let's not forget that your dear sister Lexy would be alive."

The last comment finally goaded Kyra into replying. "You aren't fit to speak her name."

"Aren't I?" A dappling of moonlight illuminated his nasty sneer. "I have no doubt that I could have seduced her too. That was my plan you know—to woo her secretly after we were wed. The idea of deflowering the pair of you was . . . exciting. But then, you went and ruined it all."

Rage boiled through Rafael's blood on hearing the cruel taunt, then turned to an ice-cold calm. He crept up close behind them, then rose from a half crouch. "Just as I shall ruin this cowardly abduction."

～

THE SOUND of Rafael's voice was like a blade of pure light piercing the blackness of her captor's malevolence. As Matherton whirled around, surprise loosened his grip for an instant, allowing Kyra to twist free.

He lunged to recapture her, only to be knocked backward by a hard punch to the face.

"My nose!" he howled as blood streamed down his chin. "You've broken my nose!"

"Yes, and I intend to break every bone in your miserable body," answered Rafael. He caught Kyra as she swayed and steadied her with a quick hug. "Are you alright, my love?" he asked. "If this miscreant has harmed you in any way, I shall also break his worthless neck."

"I'm fine," she whispered, reveling in the feel of his warm, solid body. Nothing could harm her now. "With your arms around me, I could face Lucifer and a legion of dark devils."

His lips touched her brow. "You won't ever have to face devils or demons again."

Wiping the blood from his face, Matherton scrabbled back a step, a mingling of bullying bravado and fear contorting his features. He whipped out a concealed knife from inside his coat. "Stay back," he blustered in a shrill voice. "Or I'll slash your neck from ear to ear."

"Not bloody likely." Rafael released his hold and angled his body to shield her. "Fancy yourself a warrior, Matherton? Well, let's see who has more expertise with a blade. Just a word of fair warning—point that at me and it will end up rammed down your gullet."

Matherton retreated again, waving the weapon wildly through the air. Darting a nervous glance at the dark silhouette of the bridge, he replied, "Bloody Hell, you want damaged goods? Very well, you can have her. There are plenty of other plump pigeons to pluck."

"Not for you," said Rafael calmly. "Your days as a predator are over."

"I am a titled English lord, and you are a half-breed nobody," shouted Matherton. He added a harsh laugh. "Kyra is a ruined lady, shunned by Society. Whose story do you think will be believed?"

"Lord Olivito has the most noble blood from both Spain and England running through his veins," countered Kyra. "While you have polluted any claim to honor with your evil."

Matherton's foul oath was cut off by Hero's snapping growl. Teeth bared, the hound slowly stalked closer

The knife flashed up, and with a grunt, Matherton swung a vicious blow—

BANG!

Kyra flinched, but in the momentary flare of gunpowder sparks she saw the weapon fly out of her former fiancé's hand.

Raphael lowered his pocket pistol and let it drop to the ground. "There—we're now both unarmed. Shall we go *mano a mano* as real men do?"

Clutching his hand, which had been nicked by the bullet, Matherton began babbling a mad mix of invectives and threats. "You'll both pay for this! I'll see you disgraced! I have powerful friends."

"You have nothing, save a list of sordid sins. Whatever influence you once wielded, it is over."

"No! No!" As he screamed, Matherton was crabbing toward the river and the grassy verge on the far side of the bridge, where his carriage was poised for flight. Boots slipping and sliding over the damp slope, he had just reached the path when Hero suddenly took off after him.

In a blur of starlit grey, the hound leaped, teeth gnashing, paws flailing. The impact sent them both flying into the water.

"Hero!" cried Kyra and started forward.

"Have no fear." Rafael eased her back with a gruff chuckle. "I am quite confident our *amigo* will come to no harm."

Sure enough, after a frenzy of thrashing and bubbling, the hound swam back to the near bank and clawed his way back up to the path. Clamped in his jaws was a mass of sodden fabric.

As for Matherton, he splashed through the far shallows and fell to his knees in the mud, exhausted and fighting for breath around his sobs of rage. The moon broke free from the scudding clouds, and for a moment the silver light shone bright on his naked arse.

"How apt—you are stripped of your lies, and your perfidy is now bared for all to see!" called Rafael. "Listen, and listen carefully, Matherton. You will get in your carriage and fly to the coast, where you will embark on the first ship leaving for the Continent. I own all your debts, and if you are still on English soil at dawn, I will have you arrested and thrown into debtor's prison. If you ever set foot back in England, you will be thrown into debtor's prison. Do you understand me?"

"But I can't go to a strange country. With no money, no friends, no entrée into society, my future prospect will be ruined!"

Rafael's face looked as if it had been chiseled out of granite. "Precisely."

Kyra couldn't summon up a twinge of pity for her former fiancé. A man that rotten to the core deserved none.

"You are wasting precious time, Matherton," added Rafael. "The clock is ticking."

Dragging himself to his feet, he yanked his shirttails and coat down to cover his nakedness and hurriedly limped off.

Woof. A shower of muddy river water dampened Kyra's gown as Hero shook himself vigorously and dropped Matherton's torn trousers at her feet with a happy canine smile.

Rafael chuckled. "I think my *amigo* may have won the honors tonight for his prowess in battle."

"I think," said Kyra, "you are both the most wonderful heroes in the world."

Woof.

He tipped up her chin. This time, his embrace was long and leisurely.

"Nothing is sweeter than your kiss," she said as their lips feathered apart.

"Not even my chocolate confections?" he asked with a zephyr-soft laugh.

"No," she said decisively. "Not even chocolate."

"I shall not argue the point." Twining his fingers with hers, he glanced up at the sky. "But much as I would like to prolong our intimacies, we had better return to the Manor. It's getting close to midnight, and I have been promised a special waltz."

CHAPTER 18

"Aren't you worried?" Harriet paused in pacing the perimeter of the rear parlor to peer out the window. "Lud, do you think—"

"Never fear," counseled Jack, though his face betrayed a trace of worry. "I saw the look in Rafe's eyes before he raced off. He'll rescue Kyra if he has to thrash the Devil himself to win her back."

"Right-ho," agree Theo in an unsteady voice.

"Surely there must be something we can do?" muttered Harriet. "I hate feeling helpless."

The three of them had slipped away from the festivities to confer among themselves on whether any stone had been left unturned.

""For now, we had best let Rafe fight the enemy while we battle to keep the guests from asking too many questions," replied Jack. "Though for now, it looks like we've managed to quash any speculation."

"That was quite clever of you to think of using a lost dog as a reason for Kyra's absence. And the fact that Rafael is helping her and the gardeners search for him," said Theo.

"Yes," agreed Harriet. "But if they do not return. There is only so long that the explanation will appear plausible."

"Let us not look for trouble," advised Jack. "It is having an easy enough time finding us as it is." He glanced at the mantel clock. "Speaking of time, my abject apologies for forgetting my earlier obligations. I've reneged on my invitation to dance the first two waltzes with me."

"It doesn't matter," said Theo quickly. "We all had far more important things on our minds."

"Dancing with the most alluring ladies of the ball is *very* important," countered Jack. Catching Harriet's tiny nod at her friend, he bowed to Theo. "Midnight is approaching and the last waltz of the night will herald in the new day. Will you consent to partner me?"

"B-b-but . . ."

"No buts—our appearance on the dance floor will help distract from the fact that Kyra is still missing."

"You can ask any of the London belles here, and they would be more than happy to help you create a distraction."

Jack winked and offered her his arm. "But I'd rather ask you."

Harriet reluctantly pushed back from the window. "If there is no sign of them by morning, what should—"

"Did you hear that?" interrupted Theo. "It sounded like a bark."

They all went silent.

"There it is again," she whispered.

Whirling around, Harriet pressed her nose to the glass. "Something is moving in the shadows of the garden walkway." A pause. "Oh, thank Heavens—it's Hero!"

Theo flew to her side. "And there is Kyra and Mr. Greeley." She started to giggle. "But given the state of their clothing, I don't think they will be taking their place on the dance floor."

"You ladies are not quite as well-acquainted with Kyra as I

am." Jack grinned. "Let us hurry. I wouldn't miss this grand entrance for all the tea in China!"

~

"I CAN'T APPEAR at the highlight waltz of evening looking like something the cat dragged backwards through a bramble bush," protested Kyra. She paused on the terrace, listening to the sounds of laughter and clinking crystal float out through the arched windows. Through the leaded panes, she could see that the ballroom was ablaze with a myriad candles, the brilliant flickers illuminating the colorful whirl of silks and glittering jewels.

"You've never looked more lovely," said Rafael, picking a twig out of her hair. "And besides, we can blame it on the dog."

Hero sat back on his haunches and pricked up his ears.

"We'll send Hero in first." The hound's scraggly fur was still damp and matted with weeds and mud. "No one will think to quibble over a few rips or streaks on your silk."

"You're impossibly mad," she said, watching the starlight sparkle like dancing diamonds on the tips of his dark lashes. "And impossibly wonderful."

His smile took another sinuous little curl. "Hero deserves some of your Cook's special liver pate. And you and I deserve a glass of champagne." He held out his hand. "Shall we?"

She let out a soft laugh. "I think that at this moment, I would say yes if you suggested we fly to the moon on silver-winged unicorns."

"No unicorns," he said. "Just me and a smelly dog to escort you into the ballroom."

Their fingers entwined. "Fairy tale enchantments are all very well, but the real magic is right here beside me."

"Lead the way, *amigo*," said Rafael with a wave at the hound.

Tail wagging, Hero made for the French doors of the side saloon and nosed them open. He sniffed the air expectantly, then trotted straight through the entrance foyer leading into the ballroom.

A few shrieks sounded as he brushed past a gaggle of turbaned matrons, but after a moment of shocked silence, a wave of laughter rolled through the crush of guests. Claws clicking on the polished parquet, the hound gamboled around in a ragged circle in the middle of the dance floor before catching the scent of the supper room and racing for the side door.

"Be sure to fix our four-footed friend a large plate of pate and beefsteak," said Rafael to one of the liveried footmen. "He's had a very eventful evening and deserves it." Taking two flutes of champagne from the fellow's tray before he hurried off, Rafael handed one to Kyra. "A toast," he said. "To the future, my love, now that the past will never come back to haunt you."

Lifting her glass, Kyra looked over the rim into his blue eyes, their sapphirine hue glittering in the candlelight, beckoning her to leave all darkness behind her.

"To the future," she repeated.

"Ah, there you are my dear!" The duke made his way through the crowd paused to survey the smiling couple. "I see you have found your Hero," he added, a mischievous twinkle coming to life in his eyes.

"Yes, I have, Papa." Her lips quirked. "It wasn't easy, but Mr. Greeley was kind enough—and patient enough—to offer his assistance. I couldn't have done it without him."

"My heartfelt thanks, sir," said her father loudly. "And how fortuitous that the two of you made it back in time for the midnight revelries." His brows rose ever so slightly. "I have a special surprise announcement to make. I am sure that you and my daughter would have been very disappointed to miss it."

"Very, Your Grace," agreed Rafael with a straight face. "Perhaps you could show me to a private parlor where I might brush the worst of the dust from my clothing."

"An excellent suggestion. Follow me."

"I'll fetch a bowl of water and a towel." Jack cut a path through the sea of smiling faces for Harriet and Theo. "You appear to have bloodied your knuckles."

Rafael flexed a fist. "So I have. But no lasting damage done—to my hand, that, is."

Jack grinned. "I'm delighted to hear it." To the musicians seated in the gallery he added, "We shall be back in a trice. Don't you dare start the music without us."

"I am sure you would like to freshen up as well," Harriet said. "Though I must say, that's a very pretty hue of moss clinging to your hem."

"Harry," hissed Theo. "She looks lovely just as she is."

"Of course she does. Love makes any lady beautiful beyond words." Harriet hooked her arm through Kyra's and lowered her voice to a whisper. "But if we retire to the withdrawing room, we can hear all about the evening while we pluck off the ferns stuck to the back of her skirts."

Theo's face split into a wide grin. "Oh, right-ho. Can't spin through an engagement waltz with ferns clinging to your derriere."

RAFAEL WATCHED Kyra return from the salon corridor, flanked by her two beaming friends. The candles in the chandeliers still flickered just as before in the night breeze, and yet the room seemed suffused with an ethereal golden glow. Glancing upward at the vaulted decorative ceiling, he sent up a silent prayer of thanks to Dona Maria. It was, he knew, her sweet confections that had helped to rekindle Kyra's appetite for life.

And my own.

Jack nudged his arm. "You're a damn lucky fellow. I hope you know that."

He smiled.

"And if you ever forget it, it's *your* nose that will be bloodied."

Kyra leaned in to exchange a whisper with Harriet and both of them laughed. He felt his heart lurch and thump against his ribs. "No danger of that, Jack."

The candles flickered overhead, and for a moment his cousin looked a little pensive. But before he could say more, the duke climbed up to the musician's gallery and held up a hand for silence.

The guests stilled in anticipation.

"As you know, I've promised the announcement of an engagement."

Glances darted between Kyra and Jack, then lingered on Rafael.

Clearly enjoying himself, the duke let the pause draw out.

"Don't keep us in suspense, Your Grace," called out one of his neighbors.

Pierpont chuckled. "Very well. I am happy, nay, I am absolutely delighted, to announce that Hendrie's nephew, Mr. Greeley, has asked for my dear daughter's hand in marriage, and she has accepted."

A cheer went up.

"And so, I propose a toast." The duke raised a bottle and popped the cork, much to everyone's amusement as foam fizzed up, wetting his cheeks. "To . . . To . . ."

"To family and friends—and to love, the force that ties us all together," suggested Jack.

"Since when did that young jackanape become a poet?" quipped Pierpont, eliciting another round of laughter.

In response, Jack signaled the orchestra to strike up the music. "I can summon some semblance of civilized behavior on occasion." He took Theo's hand and led her out to the dance floor. A second gesture beckoned Rafael and Kyra to come to take their place on the center rosette. They were quickly followed by the duke, with Harriet as his partner.

As the first chords of the music rose to fill the room, Rafael drew Kyra close, reveling in the warmth emanating from her being. "Nothing in this world," he breathed, "is sweeter than having you in my arms."

"Your kiss comes close." Kyra smiled. "So does your champagne truffle."

"On second thought . . ." He leaned in to press his lips to her cheek. "We may have to explore a number of different sensations before coming to a final conclusion."

Laughter pooled in her eyes, along with an undercurrent of passion that made his pulse begin to pound. "I look forward to that, my love. My than words can say."

OTHER

OMNIBUS

Christmas by Candlelight

ABOUT THE AUTHOR

I started creating books at the age of five, or so my mother tells me. And she has the proof—a neatly penciled story, the pages lavishly illustrated with full color crayon drawings of horses and bound with staples—to back up her claim. I have since moved on from Westerns to writing about Regency England (clearly I have a thing for Men In Boots!) a time and place that has captured my imagination ever since I opened the covers of Jane Austen's "Pride and Prejudice."

I have a BA and an MFA in Graphic Design from Yale University, where I studied book design (As you see, I've always had a left brain-right brain love affair with art and the printed word.) These days, when I'm not tethered to my keyboard I enjoy traveling to interesting destinations around the world—however, my favorite spot is London, where the esoteric museums, funky antique markets and used book stores offer a wealth of inspiration for my stories.